BLOW, BUGLES, BLOW

Blow, Bugles, Blow

by

MERRITT PARMELEE ALLEN

DECORATIONS BY ALAN MOYLER

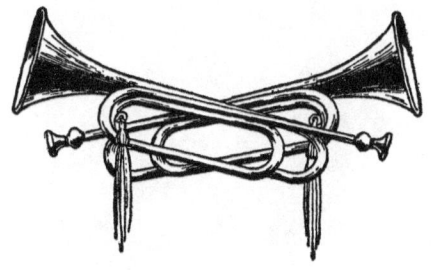

WILDSIDE PRESS

☆ 1 ☆

JUDGE MEADER WORE A LONG-TAILED COAT. IT GAVE HIM A look of distinction in keeping with his reputation of being the best lawyer in the Mohawk Valley and a friend of President Abraham Lincoln. But he was also the friend of all boys, especially the wiry, black-eyed youngster of eighteen or so who sat on the opposite side of the big office desk.

"Rick," the judge said, as man to man, "you are in a fix."

"I know it, Judge." The boy looked him in the eye.

"Yes, sir, in a fix. You are guilty of rifling a strongbox and stealing a horse. Those are serious offenses."

"But, Judge, you just told me I did right."

"No, no, no! I never said that, Rick. I said you had provocation, but that doesn't make it right in the eyes of the law."

"I did what I thought was right."

"I am sure you did. Perhaps this is the first time you have been up against the fact that under certain circumstances a man cannot obey his conscience and the law."

"Anyway, I did it, so I guess it means jail for me." The

boy clenched his fists on the desk. "I am not sorry for what I did to the Pottses. I wish I'd done more while I was at it. I'll take my medicine. And I'll go now, Judge. I haven't a dollar, but some day I'll pay you for explaining the law to me. That's all I can do now." He stood up, not very tall, but straight in his cheap clothes.

"What about counsel, Rick?"

"You mean hire a lawyer to fight for me?" The boy shook his head. "I haven't a copper, nor the prospect of one, now you say the colt doesn't belong to me."

"Have you any relatives you might call on in a pinch?"

"No, sir. You remember when my folks died that winter. I was six. The Pottses took me in. Ma Potts was all right, but she's gone now. I hate Mr. Potts and Ed — especially Ed."

"You won't have a chance without a lawyer, Rick."

"Nor with one, from what you say. They've got me, Judge."

"We might surprise them."

"We?" The boy caught at the word.

"Yes. Just between ourselves, Rick, I don't love the Pottses either. Let's fight them together, eh?"

"But, sir, I can't afford it."

"I can. Do I get the case?"

"Yes, if you will trust me till I earn the money. I don't know when that will be." The boy's tanned face flushed with eagerness.

"Agreed." The judge turned to his desk. "Now to business. You have given me the gist of your story, but I want it in chronological detail."

"I don't know what you mean by that," Rick said honestly, sitting down by the desk.

"Step by step, in the order in which it happened. When did the trouble start?"

"Three days ago, when Ed got his draft call. He was scared stiff, though he's twenty-one. His father is ripping mad at the government."

"Not a noble example to set his son," the judge commented.

"After he had ranted for a while he ordered me to go as Ed's substitute. He said it doesn't matter that I am three years younger than Ed. First he offered me a hundred dollars bounty."

"The usual price is three hundred."

"He finally upped it to that. But I won't fight that — that skunk's battles." Rick flushed. "I won't fight anybody's battles just for money. I've wanted to enlist ever since the war started three years ago, but I won't be bought."

The judge eyed him a moment thoughtfully. "Then what happened?"

"When old — when Mr. Potts heard that, he said, seeing as he has been my guardian since my folks died, he could force me to go as Ed's substitute. I told him he was a liar — that is, I told him he couldn't do it. The war is being fought to free slaves. He can't make a slave of me."

"Obviously," the judge agreed.

"Then he said if I wouldn't go for Ed I couldn't go as a volunteer. I'd have to stay and work on the farm so we — that is, he — could make more money." The boy's lips tightened. "I was mad and I told him I was through. I was going to take my colt and clear out."

"That was the day before yesterday, but you did not leave until today?" The judge watched him closely.

"I couldn't get hold of the paper till today," Rick answered.

"Be more specific about that paper, Rick."

The boy thought for a few moments, then he said, "When Ma Potts died I figured I'd run away. Mr. Potts was my guardian, but that was so he could have the right to keep me working all the time for nothing. The old man knew what was in my mind so he told me I could have my pick of the colts on the farm when I was eighteen, if I worked till then. I love horses, Judge."

"I know you do, Rick."

"So I agreed to it and we signed that paper. I was eighteen last week, just when Ed got his draft call. I claimed the colt, but the old man said I couldn't have it till I was twenty-one. I asked to see the paper we had signed and he wouldn't let me have it. I thought I had a right to the paper, so this morning, when he went to town and Ed was up in the back pasture, I pried open his tin box and I took it."

"Thereby violating the law," the judge said sternly.

"I know that now. Pretty quick Ed came along and, just

to be mean, started throwing stones at my colt. I pitched into him and gave him a darn good licking. I'm glad I did. Then I rode the colt here to show you the paper."

"Which, technically, was horse stealing, Rick."

"But, Judge, I thought the colt was mine."

"I know you did. But what a person thinks is not always what the law says." The judge picked up a paper from the desk. "This document is cleverly worded. It says you are free to choose a colt when you are eighteen, but it does not become your property until you are twenty-one."

"I'm no good at understanding things," Rick said miserably. "There's no use your wasting time on me, Judge. I'm not worth it. I'll take my medicine and go to jail. I — I wanted to enlist, but they wouldn't want a big fool like me." He stood up and doubled his fists, but for all that tears stood in his eyes. However, the eyes were steady. "Anyhow," he added hotly, "I'm glad I whaled Ed."

"Yes, that was deeply gratifying." The judge smiled slightly. "Now to resume. About what time today did you and Ed have your fight?"

"Early in the forenoon. I came right here and have been waiting to see you. I thought then I could sell the colt and pay you for your advice, but that's all knocked in the head now." Rick bit his lip.

"Young man," the judge said severely, "your case is in my hands and I don't fancy being told repeatedly it is hopeless."

"I'm sorry, Judge."

"Have you been to dinner?"

"No, sir."

"Here is a dollar."

"But, Judge . . ."

"I am your attorney and I expect you to follow my instructions. Eat at a hotel or pick up some crackers and cheese in a store."

"I wouldn't know how to act in a hotel," Rick said.

"Then run along. Come back when you have eaten."

For the first time in his life Rick bought a meal. Cheese, doughnuts and a smoked herring might be mean fare for some, but the thrill of making his own selection and paying for it over the counter made him giddy with independence. Suddenly, for a few minutes, he had the power to impose his will on another person, to tell the clerk in the store what he wanted and to get it without question. When he added five cents' worth of candy he knew the joy of reckless extravagance. He was having one glorious fling before they put him in jail.

He swaggered down the street, eating the candy, unconscious of the March wind and feeling less like a Potts' chattel every minute. He was taking a long step toward manhood.

"There he is! There's the thief!" Ed Potts' big voice brought Rick out of his reverie.

Ed, his father, and Fred Mack, the sheriff, were coming up the street. Rick stopped where he was because the thought of giving ground before those Pottses was repugnant to him. He had done so in days gone by, he never would again.

"Horse thief!" Ed roared, the words whistling between his widely spaced yellow teeth.

"Grab him, Fred," Potts commanded. He was thin, with unhealthy skin the color of muddy water that had frozen. "He's a thief and a robber, and he beat up my boy here."

"Quite a fellow," the sheriff said mildly. "Seein' as he's 'bout half the size of Eddie, he's quite a fellow."

"He took me when I wasn't lookin'," Ed explained.

"That's a lie," Rick shot at him.

"You shut up," Potts snapped. "Jail him, Fred."

"I've got to do it, Rickert," the sheriff said, with honest regret. "Later, we'll rig you up with a lawyer."

"I've got a lawyer," Rick said.

"Got a lawyer before you're even arrested?"

"Judge Meader has my case."

"Well, I swan!" The sheriff's eyes widened.

"It isn't legal to hire a lawyer till after a criminal's been jailed," Potts protested, plainly disturbed.

"That'll be decided in the courthouse, not on the street," Mack said, in a tone that might have been construed as anti-Potts.

"Besides," Potts added, "he hasn't a cent to hire a lawyer."

"Of course he hasn't," Ed sneered. "We gave him everything he ever had."

"But I gave you that shiner you're wearing," Rick lashed out. The discoloration under Ed's left eye added nothing attractive to his fat, stupid face.

"You see, he owns up to being guilty of battering Eddie," Potts said. "Now go along to jail with him, Fred. Folks're beginning to look at us on the street."

"Some folks'll gawp at anything," the sheriff remarked. "Oh, well, come along, Rickert."

"Judge Meader told me to come back to his office, Mr. Mack." Rick did not move.

"Then we'll have to go." Mack was obviously relieved. "A judge has more say in such matters than a common deputy sheriff."

"You can't do that, he's under arrest," Potts cried.

"The judge is?"

"The boy, you fool."

"Careful of your language toward officers of the law," Mack said coldly. "Rickert, you and I will walk along to the judge's office."

They all climbed the stairs, their leather boots throwing off a shower of sound from the bare boards. Rick opened the door and they filed in, Ed coming last and banging the door after him. The judge, sitting behind the big desk, frowned at that.

"Good afternoon, gentlemen," he said, in his professional tone. "What may I do for you?"

Then the story was repeated. Potts did most of the talking, picturing Rick as a criminal and an ingrate who had profited nothing by the example of his tender benefactor.

"You can't deny it, Judge," he shouted, hitting the desk with his fist. "You can't deny it."

"I neither affirm nor deny it," the judge said calmly.

"Well, what are you going to do about it?"

"Defend my client."

"In court?"

"Certainly. Where else?"

"Tell a jury what kind of fellow Rick is?"

"Yes, and what kind of fellows you and your son are."

Without batting an eye Potts changed his tune to one of gentle pity. "Judge," he wheedled, "neither me nor Eddie can bear to see this little boy branded as a criminal. For years we've used him like one of our own folks. Now we'll give him one more chance. If he'll go into the army as Eddie's substitute we'll let bygones be bygones."

"No!" Rick jumped up. "I'll never fight Ed's battles for him. He's a coward or he'd have enlisted long ago."

"That's talking!" the sheriff said heartily.

"I'm no coward." Ed made a ludicrous attempt to look brave.

"You are!" Rick glared at him. "You're a big sniveling coward."

"All right." Potts' dirty brown beard trembled. "You've had your chance, now you go to jail."

"A moment, if you please, gentlemen," the judge said in a friendly tone. "Before taking further action I ask permission to speak to my client privately."

"Go ahead," the sheriff said.

Rick followed the judge into an inner office.

☆ 2 ☆

THE POTTSES WERE DISSATISFIED WITH THE WAY THINGS were going and glared at Sheriff Mack. He ignored them, which increased their resentment.

"You're no kind of officer," Potts finally burst out.

Mack made no comment.

"He didn't hear you, Pa, or else he's tryin' to be sassy," Ed said in an aside.

"An officer who takes sides in cases is a disgrace to the country," Potts said more loudly.

Mack gave him a long look and asked, "What country?"

"The United States, pretty likely."

"Oh. I thought by the way you and Ed have been acting for the past three years you might belong to some other country."

"We've worked hard to raise food for the army."

"It does not seem so to me. I have two boys in the army."

"I offered to hire a substitute," Ed blustered. "Rick won't go, but I'll find somebody else."

"I doubt it, Ed." The sheriff looked at him in disgust. "The country is drained dry of that kind. From now on when a man is drafted he goes. Your number has been called, Ed, and if the law and local opinion means anything, you are off to war."

"I won't go," Ed said flatly. "I'll give more'n three hundred dollars. Pa, maybe Rick'll go for five hundred. Ask him, Pa, go ask him." The big calf's eyes were wide with fear.

The sheriff turned his back. Then the door opened and Judge Meader, with a paper in his hand, came in, followed by Rick.

"Gentlemen," the judge said briskly, "permit me to introduce Private Rickert O'Shay, United States Volunteers."

"Bully for you, boy!" The sheriff grabbed Rick's hand.

"He — he's enlisted?" Potts stammered.

"Yes." The judge held up the paper. "The case against him is dismissed by order of the United States."

"It's not legal," Potts said loudly.

"Let him go, Pa," Ed said sullenly. "I'll get myself a substitute and I won't pay no long price neither. Rick's sold his pigs to a poor market."

The sheriff caught Rick's arm as he swung at Ed. The judge opened the door suggestively and father and son clumped down the stairs.

Rick looked about the room. He was now a Union soldier! One of Abe Lincoln's army! It had been his dream for three years and now in his innocence he believed there was nothing but glory ahead.

"That's what I call quick work, Judge." The sheriff's lined face relaxed in a smile.

"Something like the old days, eh?" The judge wiped his

glasses. "Rick is the first volunteer I have seen for a year — a breath of fresh air after dealing with conscripts and substitutes and bounty-jumpers."

"The cream has been skimmed off," Mack said sadly. "Makes a man wonder how much health there is in skimmed milk."

"The cream still rises," the judge said heartily.

"Reminds me of when my boys — but never mind." The sheriff swallowed hard. "Yessir, Rickert, you're in the army and you wasn't dragged in by the collar. We're proud of you."

Rick blushed clear behind his ears and tried to cover his embarrassment by asking in a businesslike tone if signing his name was all there was to enlisting. The judge told him that was the main thing. Somewhere along the line he might be given a physical examination, a mere formality. If a fellow looked like anything but an invalid and was not too old, they asked no questions.

"Have I lost the colt, sir?"

"I am afraid so, Rick. But you couldn't have taken him with you."

"I want to join the cavalry. I saw a bunch of cavalry go through here once, the band played and the girls gave cookies to the men. Besides, I like horses."

"When did you see that troop go through?" Mack asked.

"Almost three years ago. Old Potts wouldn't let me see many soldiers for fear I'd run away. And he wouldn't let me read much in the newspapers."

"I wish you would skip downstairs and get me a paper."
The judge tossed Rick a coin.

"Sure." The boy was off.

"Potts has kept him in virtual slavery. It is high time he
was freed. The army will educate him or kill him," muttered the judge.

"That's a hard thing to say."

"I know it." The judge looked suddenly tired. "Three
years ago I wouldn't have said it."

"It's the same all over, North and South," Mack said.

"That makes it worse, Fred. We are one people."

Mack wiped his forehead. "Who's right and who's
wrong don't make so much difference now as when will it
end? How much longer can any of us stand it, Judge?"

"Ask Abraham Lincoln — as he hangs there on the
cross."

"A lot of us hang with him." The sheriff thought of his
two boys.

Rick came up the stairs whistling. He opened the door
and held out the newspaper. His eyes shone and his face
was bright with happy excitement.

"The paper says General Grant has everything fixed to
lick the Johnnies as soon as the spring mud dries up. Gosh!"
He caught his breath. "I hope I get in before it's over."

"You see, Fred," the judge said.

Rick spent the night at Judge Meader's home. It was a
fabulous place of carpets — the first ones the boy had ever
stepped on — upholstered furniture, silver tableware and
quiet, friendly conversation. One room was lined with

books, and he saw Mrs. Meader reading. A woman reading a book! Rick sensed, rather than understood, that when he stepped out of the judge's inner office he had entered a new world. From now on everything would be different. If he had known the lessons that were ahead and how he was to be taught, he would not have slept so peacefully in the big bed.

In the morning the judge advanced him two months' army pay, twenty-six dollars, an inexhaustible fortune to the boy.

"Take good care of it," the judge warned. "You will meet some tough customers."

"Do soldiers steal?" Rick asked incredulously.

"I regret to say some do."

"But a man who fights for his country has to be all right, doesn't he?"

They were walking down the street toward the depot and the judge jingled the contents of a pocket before he answered, "Son, a uniform doesn't make a man."

"I was thinking of Union soldiers, sir."

"So was I. Some of the lowest creatures wear Union uniforms. Some of the finest wear Confederate gray, and vice versa. You will find that a man is a man regardless of the color of his coat. Watch your comrades closer than you do your foes. You and the enemy fight face to face, but a friend may stab you in the back."

Rick heeded none of this advice at the time. He was as ignorant of the world as a person could be and knew just enough not to realize how little he knew. During the past, few hours the farm drudge had become the companion-in-arms of U. S. Grant and he was in no state of mind to be told he was not a superior being.

"Don't worry, Judge Meader," he said cockily, "I can take care of myself."

The judge reserved comment. The railway station was all but deserted, which was the first jolt Rick received. As he told Sheriff Mack, who sat on a baggage truck, he had heard a company of recruits was coming on the next train from Buffalo.

"Yeh, they'll be along." Mack swung his feet in a bored way.

"Won't there be a band here?"

"Oh." Mack glanced at the judge. "No, I don't think there'll be a band out this time."

Rick was disappointed, but cheered up, showing Mack his money.

"Don't do that," the sheriff said sharply. "Put that stuff inside your shirt and don't parade it to anybody."

The locomotive whistle blew. Rick stuffed the money in his pants pocket and ran to the edge of the platform. A few people appeared, but he saw only the smoking, roaring giant that had come to take him away.

"Wait till the cars stop." The sheriff caught his arm.

Rick saw a stream of men's faces behind the windows. "Where are they all going?" he asked.

"To blazes, most of 'em," Mack answered.

The train stopped with a jerk and a man in a blue uniform came down the steps of the last car. Perhaps he is the band leader, Rick thought. No, he is a soldier, an officer by the looks of him. It was nice for him to come out to speak to a recruit. Rick grinned and waved a hand to show he appreciated the attention.

The officer ignored him. "Another lamb for the slaughter?" he said to Judge Meader, who had come up.

"A bona fide volunteer, Jim."

"Well! Just when we thought the species extinct. Papers in order?"

"Yes." The judge handed him an envelope. "I attended to them myself to facilitate action."

"Good!" The officer seemed to notice Rick for the first time. "In you go," he ordered sharply, but not unkindly.

"The best of luck, Rick!" The judge squeezed the strong brown hand.

"Thank you, sir." Of a sudden the boy felt sort of empty.

"Better than the best." Mack slapped his shoulder. "You're a good rooster, Rickert."

"Thank you, Mr. Mack."

Officer and boy entered the car and the train puffed away.

The sheriff bit his mustache. "He's so little and so green! It's a sin to send him into that hell down there."

"I know it, Fred." The judge blew his nose.

"The worst of it is . . ." The sheriff stopped abruptly.

"Stop that train!" The telegrapher was running down the platform, waving his arms at the disappearing smoke. "Stop that train!"

☆ 3 ☆

RICK ENTERED A RAILWAY CARRIAGE FOR THE FIRST TIME
in his life. He was prepared for something unusual, but not
for what he saw. Sprawling on the seats and lying in the
aisle were about thirty men, every one of them dirty and
mean-looking. The dregs of Great Lake ports, thieves,
gamblers, murderers, bums of every degree of depravity,
they had sold themselves for a bounty or had been forcibly
drafted into the army. Some of them were bounty-jumpers,
men who made a business of enlisting for pay and then
deserting to a part of the country where they were unknown, there to enlist again. In one package were the glaring
products of the most vicious form of military service ever
practiced by a free nation.

A soldier with a musket stood inside each door. Their
faces were hard, for they were veterans who despised these
vermin.

"Sit down!" the nearest one barked as Rick entered.
Then he noticed the smooth young face and asked, "Sure
you're on the right train, bub?"

"I — I guess so. I'm a soldier."

"Drummer boy?"

"No, soldier."

"Lie if you want to, it's your funeral. Sit down."

As the train started Rick slid into a hard, narrow seat and stared wide-eyed out the window. The glass was filthy, but to the boy it sparkled like magic crystal. The fields beyond were muddy and tortuous to traverse, yet the train was whizzing along faster than a horse could run. It could keep it up for hours without effort by man or beast.

"Gosh!" Rick said aloud. "Ain't it wonderful!"

"Heh?" A porcine sound came from beside him. His seatmate, a bloated, shifty-eyed fellow, cackled, "What's so nice? Goin' toward the war'n enjoyin' the ride! You can't have no brain a-tall."

"You can't have any guts, if that's the way you feel," Rick retorted.

"You little stinker!" The man clenched a grimy fist.

"Who do you think you are, mister?" Rick demanded.

"Listen." The other's tone was low and vicious. "Be you planted here?"

"I don't know what you mean."

"This." A knife slid in sight from beneath the ragged coat. "If you try to start something, you'll get it."

"Put that up or I'll call the guard," Rick said, trying to sound calm and experienced.

"Sure." The knife disappeared. "But remember what I told you."

Rick sat at the far end of the seat wondering what he should do. The man might be drunk or insane, though he looked to be a tough customer in possession of his senses. What was more, he seemed to harmonize with the other passengers. Some were thin and some were fat, others were light or dark, two of them looked as stupid as Ed Potts, but every one of them had a crafty look. There was not an honest face to be seen or a frank word or snatch of laughter to be heard. Even their gestures and the positions of their bodies were somehow dishonest.

Obviously these were jailbirds under guard, yet the judge and the sheriff had said they were recruits on their way through Albany to the front. Then it came to Rick that there was a mistake in trains and those fellows were Confederate prisoners, for at that time he believed every Southerner was a villain.

"Say, mister," he asked guardedly, "are you a Reb?"

The man gave him a long slant-eyed look. "No, I am not," he finally answered. "But I wish I was. It would be fun to murder a lot of Yanks I know and get paid for it."

"I swan!" Rick said incredulously. "If you're not on either side, who are you for?"

"Shut your trap," the other snarled. "You're not so simple as you pretend." The knife showed again significantly.

Rick felt afraid of these men. He thought of complaining to the guard but why squeal before he was hurt? It was none of his business who they were or where they were going and he tried to forget them. That was rather easy to do inasmuch as the train was roaring down the valley at a

speed that thrilled him. He had heard the things sometimes traveled thirty miles in one hour and now he believed it.

There had been cultivated fields for miles, but now there
was scrubby pasture that reached back to woods. The track
was up a hill and the engine worked so hard Rick unconsciously curled his toes to help it pull. As the train crossed
the ridge and began coasting down the other side, there was
a grinding jerk as though the earth had stopped turning
beneath the wheels. Rick banged against the seat in front
and hung on as the car turned on its side.

It did not go fast nor far over, and its occupants might
have left by the doors without panic, but yelling at the top
of their lungs, they smashed the windows on the upper side
and went through headlong. The guards shouted something,
then two shots spat out. There was a high-pitched scream
and the voices scattered in all directions. A third shot — a
fourth — the locomotive's bell clanged in alarm. Someone
roared, "Shoot to kill!"

The command was superfluous. As Rick skidded along
the aisle and out on the tilted platform he saw his recent
seatmate stretched beside the track, blood pouring from
his face, the knife still in his right hand. A man in a beaver
hat lay near by, obviously unhurt but scared half to death.
Another glance showed Rick that three coaches were derailed and men, women and children were pouring out of
them. Beyond the fence about two dozen men were running
for the woods. One hung limply on the fence, his fingertips

touching the ground. The two guards stood on the embankment calmly reloading, skillful from long practice. They
fired, one after the other, and a man in the front rank of
fugitives pitched headlong, screaming.

The others ducked like rabbits. About half of them lost
their nerve, stopped, then faced about with their hands over
their heads. The guards ignored them and kept on shooting.
Together they brought down five before the remaining dozen
or so disappeared in the woods.

"It was a train robbery," the man in the beaver hat
panted, raising his head turtle-fashion. "But we beat them
off."

"They weren't robbers," Rick said, trying to think
straight. "They were running away."

"Escaped prisoners, do you think?" Beaver-hat got to his
knees.

"Looks that way. But they said they were soldiers. What
do you make of it?"

"I am studying the situation." Beaver-hat got up and
walked off at a dignified gait.

Rick stood where he was, for he could see better up there
and, besides, he didn't know what to do. People were buzzing about the derailed cars like bees whose hive had been
overturned. One woman had fainted and two others were
preparing to as soon as they were sure of an audience. The
train crew now stood by the guards, who, with rifles ready,
waited for the returning rioters.

"Over the fence and line up at the foot of the bank," one

soldier ordered. "And stay there, unless you want an ounce of lead."

They obeyed, more disgusting than ever in their cringing fear.

"I was only tryin' to ketch one fer you, Cap'n," one whined.

"Shut up!" the soldier barked.

"Conductor," the other guard asked, "when will the next train be along?"

"In about an hour," answered the one Rick had seen at the depot.

"Send a messenger to the nearest station. Telegraph Army Headquarters in Albany that the conscripts broke out. Eleven are loose. We are holding the others dead and alive."

"I'll attend to it." The conductor looked at his watch again.

"The wreck smells like a planned job. You'll probably find a loose rail," the guard said.

"I'll take the message for you," Rick offered.

"No, you won't." The soldier recognized him. "Get down in the ditch with the others."

"But, sir, I'm not a conscript, I'm a volunteer."

"Down there!" The guard pointed down the embankment.

It was useless and dangerous to argue. Rick went stiffly down to the fence and stood there, refusing to look at the loathed prisoners. The locomotive was not derailed and he heard it puff away with the message. The passengers were still shouting excitedly, but there was a hush when volunteer helpers brought in the dead men and laid them in a row by the track. Two others were too badly wounded to try any further running away. After a while the conductor reported he had found the loose rail. At that there was a burst of angry words from the passengers and a voice demanded that the surviving conscripts be shot on the spot.

"Keep your shirts on," one of the soldiers said. "We don't murder folks."

"But they're traitors and should be shot," the voice insisted.

"Use 'em like Rebs," cried another.

"We don't shoot unarmed Rebs, mister," the soldier roared.

Within an hour the locomotive was back, bringing a string of empty coaches and four more soldiers. As the prisoners were marched in, Rick saw the conductor and shouted, "You know I'm not one of these. You saw me with Sheriff Mack and Judge Meader."

"I did," the man agreed. "But you take orders from the army now."

The coach door banged behind Rick and the train moved away.

What kind of army was this? A fellow enlisted in good faith and was treated like a criminal. Rick hunched in his seat, his chin in his hands, picking at the situation and trying to understand it. Life on the Potts' farm had given him small opportunity to form opinions, but his mind was as eager as a hungry colt freed from a barren pasture and roaming new fields. Things had a different look. Formerly he had scorned those who wriggled out of military duty, but he had felt they were free to make the choice. Now he was not sure. If they were unwilling to defend the nation, though demanding protection from its enemies, they should be made to fight. He was glad to have the evil conscripts receive their deserts, even the dead men stretched on the floor of the baggage car. To be classed with them — that hurt.

The prisoners — for they were officially such now — got no food or water during the day. The courageous ones had escaped or died trying. The cowards were left and they whimpered disgustingly as time dragged on. They hated Rick because he looked clean and kept aloof. Anyone who was not with them was against them. They would have knifed him if the guards had not been watching. The boy knew he was in more danger than if he were in the battle line.

Toward evening the train pulled into Albany. The conscripts dodged back and forth across the aisle looking for a chance to run for it, but troops were on both sides.

"Come out one at a time, quietly," an officer ordered and opened the door at the rear of the car. It was not necessary for him to say what would happen if they disobeyed.

As they filed past, Rick saw a man's feet, only partly covered by a newspaper, protruding from under a seat. The guard said nothing then, but when the line was down the steps a yell of pain sounded inside and the skulker dashed onto the platform. The soldier followed deliberately, his bayonet lowered. As the prisoner shouldered his way in among the others for protection, blood ran down the heel of one of his shoes.

The conscripts were marched down the street between files of soldiers. A few civilians stopped to look, but there was no sympathy in their faces. In days gone by they had seen their men step proudly by, flags snapping, music playing. These soldiers had been free and eager and fine. Most of them were gone now. In their places came this rabble of thieves and cutthroats, held in line by cold steel. Rick looked hopefully at the first passers-by, then hung his head in shame.

The prisoners shuffled over the cobblestones, shrinking, cringing, cursing. Robust rogues would have swaggered and joked; these creatures lagged and whined. They were driven around a corner and up against a high stone wall that had a row of spikes along its top. The former penitentiary was the only place thereabouts that would hold the conscripts until they were shipped out in batches to the South. The gate opened, the men hesitated, saw the bayonets and went inside.

Rick hoped for a chance to state his case. This might come later, perhaps, but not at first. They were almost kicked into a long corridor and left to shift for themselves. Rick managed to be the last, for he had no wish to turn his back on the men with whom he had spent the day. He passed innumerable doors — to cells, he supposed — and went on into an immense courtyard. He gasped, for the place was full of men, hundreds of them. Some lay on the ground, others sat about playing cards, knots of them stood arguing and gesticulating, many were asleep despite the hubbub around them. And, so far as Rick could judge, every one was cut from the same piece as those who had wrecked the train. They must be indeed; because a double row of sentries lined the walls.

Rick was furiously thirsty and almost ran to a water bucket standing on an upended barrel. As he reached for the dipper a giant with black curly hair and a greasy face stepped in front of him.

"Not so fast, bucko." His voice rumbled in his chest. "You ain't paid your water tax."

"What do you mean?" Rick was afraid of him.

"When a fellow comes here he pays me a dollar before he gits any water."

"Pays you?"

"Yes — me."

"Who are you?"

"My name is Boss." And before the boy could dodge, he was knocked flat by a blow in the face.

It didn't put him out, but for a few minutes Rick was too stunned to move. During that time Boss went through his pockets and took all his money.

Anger made Rick forget his fright. "You said a dollar," he panted, sitting up unsteadily. "Give me back the rest of it."

"Aw, please don't make me do it," Boss mocked, and the men who had gathered around roared at the joke.

One of them who had been on the train that day pointed a finger at Rick and yelled, "He's planted to spy on us. He's in army pay."

There was a hush, then Boss asked softly, "What have you to say to that, bucko?"

Rick got up and stood with his feet wide apart. "I'm not a spy."

"What about bein' in army pay?"

"Sure I'm in the army. I volunteered and I'm proud of it."

"We don't like fellows who brag about bein' volunteers," Boss said in the same soft voice.

Rick felt sick, for he was sure the man would kill him.

☆ 4 ☆

MURDER WOULD HAVE BEEN EASY TO GET AWAY WITH IN
that place — a quick stab before the distant guards knew
what was happening, a solid front of lies afterward. Loyal
to nothing and no one, the men were united against the
hated army. A few might have objected to having a boy put
away by a bully twice his size if he had not declared himself a volunteer. When he did that he became their personal enemy.

Rick grabbed the heavy water dipper and brought it down
with all his strength on Boss's big hawk nose. The blow
was so quick and nicely delivered on that sensitive spot that
the giant folded up.

"You must be a farm boy," said a quiet voice behind
Rick. "That's just exactly the place to hit a mad bull."

Until then no one had paid much attention to the man
beside the water bucket. He was not conspicuous in a crowd,
being short and thin and middle-aged.

"I wouldn't hit him again." He held Rick's arm.

"He'll get me if I don't get him first." Rick's eyes were
bright with battle.

"You don't want to kill him — quite." The stranger

smiled, twisting his mouth to one side without opening his lips. "He's already bleeding like a stuck hog and soon he'll begin squealing."

"Oh!" Rick took in the other's blue uniform, cavalry boots and soft black hat with crossed sabers above the yellow cord. "You are a soldier."

"Yes."

Just then Boss came to with a groan that swelled to a roar. "I'll kill that damn volunteer!" He swayed to his feet, saw the blood pouring from his nose, and whipped a clasp knife from his pocket. "I'll kill him!"

"Silence!" The stranger was unarmed but his voice crackled with authority and his gray eyes burned almost red. "Go to the rear and dress your wounds."

"Who says so?" Boss's voice was thick with blood.

"He's a blueback," someone in the crowd warned. And several others shouted, "A blueback! A Lincoln blood-sucker! Beat him up!"

"Call the guards," Rick cried to the stranger.

"Why?" The cavalryman was eying the men, one after another. "These fellows won't make trouble."

Strangely enough, they did not. Even Boss withdrew.

"You must be an officer, sir," Rick said in honest awe.

"Private Pond. At your service." He used that same closed smile.

"But the way you handled those men!"

"Little David with his dipper had already tamed Goliath."

"Humph. If you hadn't come along they'd have made mincemeat of me. That's the truth, mister. They want to kill me because I'm a volunteer."

"So!" Pond looked him over sharply, saw how young and small Rick was, yet how wiry. Already he had proved his spirit. "Do you really want to be a soldier?"

"Sure I do. I've enlisted. I want to get into the cavalry."

"Of all the crazy notions! Why the cavalry?"

"I love horses."

"My great-aunt Abby loves horses but she'll never join the cavalry, though she is only eighty-six," Pond said solemnly. "No, a love of horses isn't all it takes to be a trooper."

"But it helps, doesn't it?" Rick asked hopefully.

"Oh, yes." Pond looked about the courtyard, twisting his florid face into little wrinkles. "This jail pen is no place for you," he finally said. "They must have put you in by mistake."

"That's what happened." Rick was eager to explain. "They told me . . ."

"We haven't time now," Pond interrupted. "Come up to Captain Parker's headquarters. He's the commandant. Shake your boots."

They quick-stepped along the corridor and up a flight of stairs into a small room, where an orderly asked their business.

"My compliments to Captain Parker," Pond said. "Ask

him if the old hoss doctor and a friend may have a word with him."

"Yes, sir." The orderly gave him a doubting look but went.

"By the way, boy, what's your name?" Pond inquired.

"Rick O'Shay, sir."

"Ricochet, eh? I can go you one jump better, mine is Kangaroo."

"I'm not joking. That is my name — Rickert O'Shay. Everybody calls me Rick."

"Captain Parker will see you gentlemen," the orderly announced.

"Did the captain say gentlemen or did you tack that on to be polite?" Pond asked gravely.

"It is customary," the orderly said stiffly.

Pond motioned Rick into another room and followed. "Private O'Shay, this is Captain Parker."

Rick saluted awkwardly — it was his first attempt — and wondered what to do next. The captain returned the salute briskly but not as if he were critical. Rick noticed how tall and thin he was and that his left leg had been replaced by a peg.

"Captain," Pond said, as though they were old friends, "I have found an honest man in this den of iniquity."

"Prove it." The captain smiled slowly.

"O'Shay is that man — a volunteer! And we thought that breed was gone forever. It will be, too, if we don't get him out of here before morning. He is here by mistake and wants to join the cavalry. He is urgently needed at the front and can get there quickest if he travels with me."

The captain looked thoughtfully at Rick and said in a half-wistful voice, "You're young."

"I am seventeen, sir," Rick answered stoutly. "I have already enlisted and Judge Meader has signed my papers. I want to get out of this place."

"Naturally." The captain continued to look at him. "It may be irregular — so many things are. Your papers will catch up with you some time. Take him along, Pond."

"Thank you, sir!" Rick wanted to shake his hand but didn't dare.

"You have done us a double favor, Captain," Pond said warmly.

"A pleasure I didn't expect to have in this place." The officer smiled wearily. "Good luck to you both."

Half an hour later they were on the boat for New York. It was a cold evening and the wind whistled down the river in no springlike manner. Rick did not notice it. The steamer entranced him even more than the train, for it floated as well as traveled, and it provided a place to walk and eat and sleep. Was there ever such a day as this had been! Excitement crowded it; everything and everybody new. Some good and some bad and yet, when there was time to think about it, all had worked out as though planned for Rick's advantage. No wonder his head was in a whirl.

"I don't know whether I'm afoot or on horseback," he confessed to Pond. They were in a great room rigged out with pictures and gold-framed looking-glasses and the furniture all padded and curlicued.

"You're pretty sure to be afoot here," Pond said. "As a rule, horses aren't favored in saloons. A saloon is to a sitting room what a Morgan is to a common horse. Do you like Morgans?"

"I don't remember that I ever saw one."

"Then you have never seen one. No one ever forgets a Morgan. Well, let's wash up and eat."

Rick noticed that Pond's ruddy face was freshly shaven and his graying sandy hair was carefully brushed. He seemed to fit into this elegant room and, for all his uniform and boots, didn't look like a trooper.

"Maybe I should shave," the boy said, as though the thought bored him.

"Turn toward the light." Pond solemnly inspected the dozen silky hairs that showed on the pink face. "It's a good idea for a soldier to look trim, but I wouldn't say you have a heavy beard."

"Then I'll just wash." Rick's heart warmed toward this man who might so easily have laughed at him. "Where's the water bucket?"

"I'll show you." Pond led the way along a passageway. "They call it a washroom." And a minute later, as the boy hesitated before the grand assortment of pitchers, towels and what not, "That yellow cake is soap. They don't use soft soap on ships because it slops over."

"Oh!" Rick breathed. Even the soap was different.

When they reached the dining room Rick stared at everything, lights, tables, food and people. By the number of tools they used, eating must be a trade with them, like shoemaking or tailoring. A Negro in a white coat appeared and the boy wondered if he could be the captain of the boat. Then he named over a long list of foods and asked what they would have, so he must be hired help. About the only thing Rick was sure of was ham and eggs, so he asked for that. As for Pond, he said without batting an eye he would have an icicle rolled in cracker crumbs and fried in deep fat.

"Suh!" The waiter stared at him.

"You heard me, boy."

"Yah, suh, but a — but it won't be no icicle iffen it fries in hot fat."

"All right." Pond sighed resignedly. "Give me a beefsteak. When I get to New York I will order a platterful of piping-hot fried icicles and eat them all."

The waiter went out with the order, probably to spread the word that there was a maniac on board.

Pond relaxed and smiled at Rick. "I'm collecting a debt. I have spent three hard years trying to help the Negro race, so now and then I let one of them help me with a minute of nonsense. Sometimes I get tired and worried; humor is grease for the wheels on the everyday grind. A soldier must have it. You will learn what I mean, Rick."

"I was never much at joking, Mr. Pond," Rick said.

"Work at it; it helps. By the way, we are both privates, so call me Ocean."

"You mean your first name is Ocean?" Rick suspected another joke.

"Yes. It's unusual, but there's a reason for it, as there is for everything, if you dig deep enough for it."

"I suppose so," Rick said.

"My father was forever bragging about the Ponds. They raised the biggest crops, had the biggest cattle, shot the biggest bears and caught the biggest fish. It wearied my mother, who was a Watkins, so when I was born she said there was going to be one thing in the family bigger than a Pond, and she named me Ocean."

"I guess you sort of inherit your jokes." Rick laughed. He felt pleasantly grown-up to be talking with a man three times his age. "Where is your home, Mr. — er — Ocean?"

"I live in Vermont more or less."

"Did you enlist from there?"

"I don't remember where I enlisted. Sometimes I remember to forget what I remember. But here comes our grub."

It seemed strange to Rick that the man could not remember his place of enlistment, but he was too hungry to think much about it. Soon he was too sleepy to think at all, though it seemed wasteful to sleep when there was so much to see.

Morning launched another day and floated him toward more experiences. Every bend in the Hudson widened his view of this new world. The sun was bright and in places the banks were green under the touch of spring. Here and there cattle were exploring the pastures and occasionally shaggy horses, that had spent the winter near haystacks, threw up their heads and snorted at the steamboat. Whenever that happened Ocean went to the rail and watched them breathlessly. Then he would turn in disgust and complain because he hadn't seen a Morgan for days.

"What's so wonderful about Morgans?" Rick finally asked.

"Morgans?" Ocean's eyes sparkled at the mention of the word. "There's as much difference between a Morgan and a common horse as there is between gold and brass."

"But why?" Rick persisted.

"You've only to see a Morgan, boy, to know what I mean. Look at the build of 'em! Not over fourteen hands high, as a rule, a short, round barrel, powerful but trim underpinning, deep chest, short, strong neck, small head wide between the eyes, big bright eyes and ears quick to prick up."

"That's a Morgan, eh?"

"On the outside. Inside, there's no way to describe 'em. They outpull, outtravel and outlast anything that wears horsehide. Safe for a child to handle, yet the very devil in battle. They were designed by the Almighty from a special pattern."

"Not quite that, I guess." Rick laughed.

"How else do you account for Justin Morgan?" Ocean was sincere about it. "Nobody knows who his parents were. About 1793 this colt showed up in northern Massachusetts and was bought by a schoolmaster, who raised him in Vermont. A whole breed of horses sprang from him, every one true to type, yet different from all other horses. How do you explain that?"

"Oh, it just happened," Rick said wisely.

"Such things don't just happen, boy," Ocean said, with intense earnestness. "That horse had something no other horse ever had. Everybody saw he was different — better. In 1817 there was a big celebration up in Burlington, Vermont. There were hundreds of horses in the parade, but the minute President James Monroe set eyes on Justin Morgan he stopped the show and asked permission to ride him up the hill to the speaker's stand. After he made his speech the president bowed to Justin Morgan — and the old rascal bowed back!"

"I'd like to see some of that breed," Rick said eagerly.

"I'll introduce you to Rienzi. General Sheridan's horse."

"Is he a good one?"

"A good one! Boy, the general says he's worth a regiment of troops. And he means it, too, or he wouldn't have sent me clear up here to Albany for a can of horse medicine."

"General Sheridan did that?" Rick was incredulous.

"Sure. 'Ocean,' he said to me last week, 'that old chemist in Albany is the only man on earth who makes perfect saddle gall ointment. It is a secret prescription, and I must have some. There is a lot of work ahead for me and I need Rienzi's help.' "

"Did you get the ointment?" Rick asked, breathlessly.

"Yes. I am on my way back with it now. Letters did no

good, but the chemist obliged after I explained things to him."

Rick eyed him in amazement. "All that travel for horse medicine!"

"And worth it, boy. The general knows Rienzi's worth a dozen horses. What good is a cavalry horse with a sore back? The general has ordered all the old man can make, no matter how much."

"For one horse?"

"No no no! For the cavalry mounts in the Army of the Potomac. You don't know Phil Sheridan, boy. Every horse and every man in his command is his personal responsibility. My job happens to be taking care of Rienzi."

"You talk as though you know General Sheridan well."

"That might be," Ocean answered evasively.

"How come you are only a private soldier then?"

"In the army we don't question a man's individual motives," Ocean reproved gently, but very effectively.

Rick blushed with embarrassment, yet, for all that, he wished he knew more of Ocean Pond's story.

☆ 5 ☆

CHRISTOPHER COLUMBUS VOYAGED TO A NEW WORLD AND, for that matter, so did Rick O'Shay. He had heard and read fragments about the world beyond the Potts' farm, but it was not real until he saw for himself. Then the Hudson became a river full of more water than ever fell from the sky, and New York was revealed as a vast collection of things and people that would not vanish at the end of the dream. Rick and Ocean spent a night in the city and the boy trembled for his life. Perhaps not one of those people would harm him, but the visual impact of the thousands forever in motion made him dizzy. He closed his eyes and lay back in one of the deep chairs in the hotel parlor.

"Ocean Pond! I haven't seen you for three years."

Rick partly opened one eye and saw an elderly gentleman holding out a hand. Ocean glanced at the boy, who seemed asleep, then drew the man out of sight behind the chairs.

"Shush, Jim! On your honor . . ." Then the voices of Ocean and his friend faded out.

Rick sat still, wondering.

"Have a nap, Rick?" Ocean asked a few minutes later.

"Sort of." Rick yawned.

"Let's go to bed. We will take an early train tomorrow. I

just glanced at a newspaper and saw that General Sheridan has reached his headquarters near Brandy Station, Virginia. He was stationed at Loudon, Tennessee, you know."

"I didn't know," Rick said.

"The first thing General Grant did when he took over the Army of the Potomac was to send for Sheridan and give him command of the cavalry. Sheridan is only thirty-four, but he'll make things hum. Mike left with the horses as I started for Albany."

"Who is Mike?"

"The general's young brother and aide-de-camp."

"You seem to know a lot of famous people," Rick remarked as they went upstairs.

"In the armies of the west, where I've been the past three years, even a common soldier knows officers like Grant and Sheridan. Or I should say, those officers know their men. There is a big difference. Well, here's our room. No more talking. A good soldier learns to get every minute's rest he can."

With so much to think about, sleep seemed a waste of time, but gradually Rick's thoughts lost substance and dissolved like clouds, leaving a clear sky of forgetfulness. He awoke to find Ocean shaving. Around the lather the man's ruddy skin resembled soft leather and his hair was fine and glinting. There was a gentleness and yet a firmness in his expression that was puzzling. He had the vigor of youth and yet, as Rick thought of time, he was old, perhaps halfway through the fifties.

His gray eyes twinkled when he saw Rick was awake and he warbled part of the words for Reveille:

"I can't wake 'em up, I can't wake 'em up, I can't wake 'em up in the morning.

I can't wake 'em up, I can't wake 'em up, I can't wake 'em up at all."

"I'm awake." Rick was out of bed. "What do you sing for breakfast?"

"That is Mess Call. This way:

Soupy, soupy, soupy, without any bean.

Porky, porky, porky, without any lean.

Coffee, coffee, coffee, without any cream."

They had a better meal than that and soon Ocean was leading the way to the railroad station, while Rick marveled how anyone could steer a course among those innumerable streets. Then, for the boy, the journey in wonderland was resumed. Philadelphia, Washington and the beautiful country between unfolded by the mile, farther and farther toward the land of blood that once was as fair as this. Having special passes, Ocean and Rick rode in coaches, but the stream of soldiers sat on backless benches in boxcars, without light or ventilation except for the holes they smashed with their musket butts. The men were so tired that when the trains stopped at stations they stretched out on the platforms and fell asleep.

At one of the stops they met three veterans going home on leave. The bottle they had been passing around was nearly empty and their spirits were high.

"Hooooo! Horse soldiers!" one whooped, noticing Ocean's uniform.

"There's a man who believes in playing safe," another cackled.

And a third taunted, "Whoever saw a dead cavalryman?"

Rick's eyes blazed, but Ocean laughed it off with, "A good many of them have died of old age waiting for the infantry to win the war."

The first soldier hurled the bottle at Ocean's head. It smashed against the side of the station and the next moment Rick lit into the man. Instantly the boy found this was not like fighting Ed Potts. A hairy fist that had been in a hundred brawls landed on his chin, and the only reason he did not go down was that the man was too wobbly to put his weight behind it. Rick shook his head and charged, swinging both hands in a fury. That time he did go down.

As he lay on his back, wondering why he could not move, Ocean came into view, poised on the balls of his feet. A right, a left, each started below the waist and met two faces that seemed waiting. A pivot, another uppercut and the third face dropped backward.

Rick was on his feet again.

Ocean held him back and smiled genially at the three soldiers, who were getting up unsteadily. "Shake a leg, bully boys. Your train is steaming up. Don't miss any of that furlough."

"We'll make m-m-mince m-m-meat of you f-first," one promised.

"Do that later, when you're sober," Ocean suggested.

"The cuss of it is," another said, trying hard to think straight, "if we was sober we wouldn't want to fight a couple of cheap horse soldiers."

The northbound locomotive gave an impatient whistle.

"That's for you, boys." Ocean waved them along. "Have a big time and come back to help us knock the fog out of the Johnnies."

To Rick's amazement, they slapped Ocean on the back before they ran unsteadily to their train and they were waving their caps at him when they disappeared.

Back on the train Ocean watched the telegraph poles go by. "Rick, there was a lot of truth in what they said."

"What!" Rick sat up indignantly.

"President Lincoln himself has repeated that joke about a dead cavalryman."

"Do you mean to tell me we are not as good as other soldiers?"

"Not a bit of it. The men are fine, but the Union cavalry has never been used as a unit. It is spread out everywhere doing picket duty and guarding wagon trains."

"And it shouldn't be doing that?" was all Rick could think of to say.

"No." Ocean thumped the window sill with his fist. "Look at our horses all worn out traipsing around on picayune duty. They should be massed in the rear, rested and ready to strike in force. That's the way the Rebs do it. Look what their cavalry has accomplished under men like Morgan and Forrest and Hampton and Stuart. See what I mean?"

"Yes," Rick said, though he knew nothing about it.

"I've heard Phil Sheridan cuss himself blue in the face about it, while the pretty boys from the east turned up their noses at his crude ideas. But now," Ocean hit the window sill harder, "now, by thunder, Grant has given him command of all the cavalry in the Army of the Potomac — ten thousand or more — and it will be used for something besides errand-boy work. If I know Little Phil, there'll be plenty of dead cavalrymen before long."

Early that evening the train pulled into the Brandy Station cavalry camp and the locomotive stood panting so wearily Rick believed he could see its sides heaving. On both sides of the track were scattered woods and everywhere, literally everywhere, were stacks of supplies, tents, horses and men. Tents were set along streets with breaks for company units. Most of them were dog tents for two men, made by buttoning together the halves each trooper carried and supporting the canvas on a ridgepole held by two upright sticks. Two old muskets with bayonets stuck in the ground worked just as well. Behind them the mounts were tied to a sort of hitching rail of rope running through iron stakes. There were hundreds of horses, thousands of horses, more horses than Rick once supposed were in the whole world.

Ocean jumped off the train and started down the first street at a fast clip. Rick followed, but he was so busy looking all ways at once that he fell behind. Mess was over and the troopers lounged about their fires. One noticed the awkward country boy in civilian clothes and let out a delighted bellow: "Hey, Rube!" Instantly every man facing that way picked it up and as others turned to look they added to the thundering chant: "Hey, Rube!" Someone found a cow bell, heaven knew where, and its clanging formed a perfect accompaniment.

Rick stopped and his face was red as an August sun. They were ridiculing him and he didn't like it. He was mad enough to fight any two of them, but not foolhardy enough to take on the whole camp. All but bursting with fury, he clenched his fists, stuck out his chin and marched after Ocean, paced on both sides by the raucous chorus: "Hey, Rube!"

After turning a corner toward the horse lines he caught up with Ocean and sizzled, "I could shoot those galoots!"

And without a trace of sympathy Ocean answered, "If you can't take a joke, you had better shoot yourself."

"But it's no joke, making fun of me because I haven't been given a uniform."

"Learn this before you are a minute older, Rick: in this army anything except sudden death is a joke."

"I enlisted to fight, not to be laughed at by those bums."

"Son," Ocean said quietly, "those boys are not bums. Most of them are veterans, all of them expect death any day, yet they laugh at it. When you can honestly criticize them you will be a better man than you are now."

"Yes, sir," the boy said.

Perhaps it was the sudden letdown from the excitement of the past few days, or the realization that he had spoken like a fool, that made Rick act as he did. Ocean was again several paces ahead. It was half dark among the trees, and impulsively the boy dodged into a deep shadow and lay on his face. He was a man now, a soldier, and yet he had to be alone for a few minutes and get hold of himself. Alone in the midst of an army of men who laughed at him. In his misery he honestly believed he did not have a friend on earth. Without knowing it, he was homesick, and there are few worse maladies.

Night came on, bringing all the unfamiliar sounds of camp, each one harrowing his tortured thoughts. He heard men laughing and singing and he hated them for being happy. When taps were sounded in one regiment after another, fainter and fainter in the distance, the sadness of it squeezed his heart with cold fingers. He longed to find Ocean, then felt sorry for himself because Ocean had made no attempt to find him. He felt persecuted and resentful at being abandoned by his only friend. Then he wondered, with a rush of fear, if he were already a deserter. If so, and he tried to run away, would he be hunted as a criminal? If he stayed in camp, would he be picked up in the morning and shot? To his terrified mind, the whole Army of the Potomac was in league against him, every man jack of them eager to pull him down.

But the horses were not that way, they were his friends. In all directions he heard noises that were reassuring because they were understandable, the stamping of hoofs and the shaking of heads, the munching of fodder and the impatient blowing, the long, contented sigh when a horse lay down. There was nothing to be afraid of in that part of the army. There, for a few hours at least, a fellow might find companionship.

It was cold without a blanket, but Rick knew it would be less so between the rows of horses. While he was thinking about it he heard a man walking near by. Something rattled like tin, a match flickered, then a steady light shone as the man lighted the lantern and took it from its hook on the limb of a tree. He was a trooper, a well-built young fellow, and there was light enough to show Rick his "pumpkin rinds," as a lieutenant's shoulder straps were called. He made the rounds, looking at each horse in one particular line as though it was his special charge, then he hung up the lantern, blew it out and walked away. Rick waited a while, then went over and lay down on some hay between two rows of horses. Feeling that he was among friends, he slept.

He awoke to a sound he had often heard on the farm, the violent thrashing of a horse in pain. He investigated and judged that one of the mounts near the end of the line was down with the colic. To make sure, he lighted the lieutenant's lantern and saw a little bay, badly bloated and groaning between bared teeth, lying broadside. That was bad, for his stomach might be ruptured from internal pressure or by this throwing himself about on the ground in his agony. The bay should be gotten on his feet and kept there.

It seemed an age to Rick before he had the horse up and backed out of line and tied to a tree, head well up. By then the poor beast was trembling all over and sweat was running down his legs and dripping from his fetlocks. "You're a good boy," Rick said, gently stroking the wet neck. "You need some medicine quick. Where is your master? I'll go find him for you. Grit your teeth, little fellow, we'll have you feeling better."

He took the lantern and went through the grove until he saw a dog tent. Obviously it had a single occupant, for only one pair of feet showed. Rick touched them with his toe and heard a growl within the tent.

"I'm sorry to wake you up, mister." Rick hesitated, not sure about military etiquette. "There's a sick horse out there."

Words this time, but still a growl: "What of it, you fool?"

"Why — why, I thought you might tell me where I can get some medicine."

"I'll tell you where you can get an ounce of lead."

"But, mister, the horse may die."

"I hope he does, and you with him. Now git!"

Rick had no idea what to do. There must be a horse guard or whatever it was called, but he didn't know where it was or how to address it. He was sure that to yell "Sick horse" in the middle of the night would not be the way to attract favorable attention. He wished he hadn't been foolish enough to run away from Ocean, but this was no time to find him and apologize. He went back to the horse and found him more bloated. His ears felt cold, a bad symptom.

"My gosh!" Rick said aloud. "I wish you could talk and tell me where to find a pound of soda. That would straighten you out."

"What's the row?" a voice asked in the darkness.

"There's a horse dying of the bellyache and nobody will help me," Rick answered.

"Let's have a look." The speaker walked into the light and Rick recognized the young lieutenant. "He is sick. Run over to the sutler's and get that soda."

"I don't know where to go. I just reached camp."

"I'll go." The lieutenant faded out.

"Bring some water and a dish to mix it in and a big strong bottle — sir," Rick called after him.

The officer knew his way around and returned with everything. Out of deference to rank, Rick let him take charge and he did it in a way that showed he knew horses. Together they pulled the bay's head over a limb, thrust a stick between his teeth and poured the soda and water down his throat. Then with bunches of hay they started rubbing him down from head to foot, one on each side.

"He breathes better," the lieutenant said, after a long while.

"Don't you think I'd better walk him around, sir?" Rick suggested.

"Yes. I'll carry the lantern for you."

"It is getting light, sir."

"So it is. I hadn't noticed. How long have we been here?"

"I don't know. It doesn't matter. We saved him."

"Is he your horse?"

"No, sir, they haven't given me a horse yet."

"You worked like that for just any horse?"

"Sure. I think a lot of horses."

"You must." The officer blew out the lantern.

As they walked the horse back and forth together in the faint light, they sized each other up. The lieutenant was not handsome, but he had a vigorous, friendly attitude that restored some of the faith in men Rick had lost the previous evening.

"Why aren't you in uniform?" he asked Rick.

"I just got here, sir."

"Haven't you been assigned to a company?"

"No, sir. I came straight from Albany with a friend who takes care of General Sheridan's horse."

"That must be Ocean Pond." The lieutenant looked at him sharply.

"Yes, sir. Do you know him?"

"I have heard of him. Why aren't you with him now?"

"I sort of got lost. I guess I'd better go look him up and get a job with the horses."

The lieutenant laughed. "You don't know much about the army if you expect a recruit to choose any job he wants. So you like horses?"

"Yes, sir. If I'm to be killed in the war I'd rather have it happen among horses. They are my friends."

"Well!" The lieutenant eyed him closely. "You're a natural, if I ever saw one. I have a brother like that. What is your name?"

"O'Shay, sir."

"Tie your horse in. It will soon be reveille."

When Rick returned he found a stranger talking with the lieutenant. Again Fate had taken hold of the farm boy and was shaping him to a new pattern.

☆ 6 ☆

At first sight, the stranger was a rather comical-looking little man about six inches shorter than the average soldier. His legs were bandy, his torso powerful and his arms so long his fingers hung below his knees. His swarthy face was set off by a heavy black mustache and an imperial, and his sharp black eyes had almost an Oriental slant. His uniform was wrinkled and mud-stained and high on his bullet-shaped head was a little black hat.

"O'Shay," the lieutenant said, without warning, "this is General Sheridan."

Holy smoke! Rick thought as he tried to pull himself together and salute as he had seen other soldiers do.

"My brother says you saved a horse last night," the general said, cutting the words out cleanly. "Thank you. You deserve a mount and I will see that you have one at once. Mike," to the lieutenant, "enroll O'Shay, issue him a uniform and a horse before night."

"But, Phil, five hundred troopers are dismounted now because we are short of horses," Mike protested.

"I know it. There would be five hundred and one if this

boy didn't know his business. O'Shay," Sheridan gave him a keen look, "you are an ideal size for a cavalryman — not over five feet six and under a hundred and thirty-five pounds. Don't grow any more."

"Yes, sir, I mean no, sir."

The general turned and walked away quickly.

Lieutenant Sheridan pulled out his pencil and field book. "I'll take your full name, age, place and date of enlistment. You may have been enrolled elsewhere but you will stay here. What my brother says goes."

"Yes, sir." Rick was ready to believe that.

When the lieutenant finished writing he slapped the book shut. "You may as well report to Ocean Pond for the present," he said. "I will get back to you later."

"Yes, sir."

"The general's tent is that one with the flagstaff in front. You will find Ocean in the rear of it with the horses."

"Yes, sir." Rick hurried off, more or less in a daze.

He wondered how Ocean would receive him. A bugle sounded and Rick saw men pouring out of the tents for roll call. They appeared so quickly that he guessed they had slept in their clothes, as indeed most of them had. They were too busy to notice him and, though he wanted to see what roll call was like, he decided not to linger. He skirted the headquarters tent, where a sentry and half a dozen officers stood looking important, and went around to the rear. There he saw Ocean holding the kind of horse he had always dreamed about but never expected to see.

The horse was coal black except for three white feet, every hair was lustrous and perfectly groomed, even his hoofs shone. He was tall, perhaps sixteen hands, and superbly built, deep-chested, short-backed, with mighty leg muscles that tapered down to slim ankles and produced foot-work of almost fantastic lightness. His neck was short, powerful and graceful and supported a majestic head. Perfection was in his delicate nostrils and ears. But his true spirit was in his eyes. They were large and far apart and shone with the very essence of intelligent courage. If ever there was a prince of horses, here it was.

Rick stood open-mouthed, possessed by admiration. General Sheridan came around the tent, raising a spray of dew-drops with his wrinkled cavalry boots. He paused to speak to Ocean, patted the horse's head, and was in the saddle. Now the picture was complete. Seated, the general was instantly transformed and looked as tall as anyone. He and his horse seemed fused in one piece, both flesh and spirit. The horse reared and pawed the air exuberantly, the general slapped down his little black hat, which was always in danger of falling off, and they were away at a gallop.

"They are a whole street parade in themselves," Rick said aloud. "Gosh! I can hear the band playing and see the flags waving."

"What's that?" Ocean faced about. "Oh, it's the prodigal son. We haven't any fatted calf for breakfast, but I can offer you a cupful of lemon juice rolled in catnip and toasted to a turn."

"What a horse!" Rick's eyes were shining. "What a horse!"

"He is Rienzi," Ocean said with simple pride.

"He's no Morgan. He's beyond any breed," Rick enthused.

Ocean smiled with one corner of his mouth. "He's larger than the average Morgan," he said, "probably not full-blooded, but he has all their traits. General Grant thinks his Cincinnati is animated rawhide, but Rienzi can cut circles round him all day and kick up his heels at taps. His walking gait is five miles an hour."

"And he likes it," Rick said. "You can tell by the way his ears prick forward. A lazy horse never does that."

"You do like horses."

"I envy you your job, Ocean. Do you take all the care of him?"

"Oh, yes, including the shoeing."

"Mister! What a responsibility. A battle may depend on Rienzi some day."

"He will be ready, he and the general. They are a great team."

"I talked with the general a few minutes ago," Rick said nonchalantly.

"Yes? Did you ask his advice about the war or did he ask yours?" However, Ocean accepted Rick's story. "That's Sheridan for you," he said. "He takes care of every man, horse, piece of equipment and pound of food.

"You'll see him everywhere, in camp, out on a march,

behind the lines gabbing with civilians. Affable enough but heaven help the poor sinner who lies to him." Ocean abruptly slapped his own mouth. "Stop chattering, Pond. It will soon be mess call. Are you hungry, Rick?"

"I could eat a boot."

"Come on, boy. We eat in messes of twelve, but there is always room for one more."

Rick was a small unit among tens of thousands, but at first he felt himself the center of the whole army. Wherever he was, men and horses were in motion around him. People were either unable or unwilling to keep still. Even at meal-times the troopers moved around the fires, getting in the way of the one whose turn it was to cook and blaming each other good-naturedly for their clumsiness. They were tolerant of the little recruit, but Rick knew his greenness would gain no special favors. He had volunteered to do a man's work, not a boy's, and they expected him to do it.

During that first meal he said nothing, just watched and listened and thought. The once cocky youngster was beginning to understand he must indeed take care of himself but he must do it cooperatively, not independently. This much he absorbed from army atmosphere.

Presently he was told plenty. Mike Sheridan rode up and, without a flicker of recognition, ordered him to report at a certain tent down the line. There a fat, sharp-eyed clerk, who looked like a raccoon, wrote something in a book and said Rick belonged in A Company, Third Pennsylvania Cavalry.

"Here, bub," Raccoon handed him a slip of paper, "give this to the Quartermaster's Department over by the railroad. They'll issue your outfit. Better ask for a pillow."

"I will sleep on my blanket," Rick said.

"You're so green it must rub off." Raccoon laughed. "The Third Pennsylvania is one of the hardest riding outfits in the army, that's why you'll need a pillow. Anybody as green as you are is too soft to last long."

"I'd last with a soft job like yours," Rick retorted.

"Say! Who are you talking to?" Raccoon flared.

"A common soldier like yourself. If you don't like it, lump it."

"Git!"

"Pooo!" Rick made a face and went out.

Within half an hour the Army of the Potomac had another man in uniform. The light-blue trousers were too long and the dark-blue jacket was too wide, but there was a belt with brass buckle that was helpful and showy. There was a load of other clothing, boots, cap, felt hat with crossed sabers, woolen shirts, cotton drawers, socks, overcoat, and a roll containing a blanket, rubber poncho and half a dog tent. There was also a metal cup, plate, knife, fork, spoon and skillet.

Rick was bewildered.

"Don't I have a mule to carry all this?" he asked the clerk.

The man, who was older, looked at the youngster sympathetically. "Wait till you add your saber, spurs, carbine, six-shooter and ammunition, then you'll have a load of about fifty pounds."

"I'm lucky to have a horse."

"And the horse is lucky to have a rider your size. The best cavalrymen are lightweights."

"Like General Sheridan?"

"I hope he is good. This war can't go on much longer."

"We won't all get shot," Rick said carelessly.

"Shooting is a small part of it, son. Four die of sickness for every one killed in battle."

"You're trying to scare me." Rick grinned. "The war is about over. Grant and Sheridan and Sherman are almost ready for the final punches. We can have confidence in those officers." He spoke knowingly, having heard someone talk in New York.

The clerk answered quietly, "I have confidence in only one officer — Robert E. Lee. He never makes mistakes."

"A Yank says that!" Rick stared at him.

"There is not a man on either side who doesn't believe it, way down in his heart."

"I don't."

"You will, son, you will."

Rick had no time to speculate on such thoughts. A sergeant, who regarded all recruits as lumber to be hewn to a mark, literally barked his duffel into a dog tent, then barked him out to a certain horse.

"He's yourn," the noncom said, as though the boy were guilty of crime. "If you don't take good care of him, I'll kick you so full of holes your hide can't be used for patchin' leather."

"Yes, sir."

"You got a pull somewheres to git yourself a horse. Hundreds of men're waitin' for mounts." The sergeant chewed tobacco viciously. "Smart alecks like you are only fit for the infantry."

"Yes, sir."

"But no knock-kneed, spindle-legged, flat-footed, gander-gutted, holler-chested woodenhead like you'll last long anywheres. You got a name?"

"I am Rick O'Shay, sir."

"Sass me and I'll ricochet you so high you won't git back for a week. What's your name?"

"Rickert O'Shay, sir."

"It'll look real purty on a gravestone."

There were times during the next two weeks when Rick thought it would be there, whether it looked pretty or not. Because there were more veteran troopers than horses, there was no mounted drill for recruits only, and he found himself taking part in evolutions he had never heard of before. It was like being taught to swim by being thrown into deep water.

If curses and ridicule had had specific gravity he would have sunk. The men loved to haze a greenhorn and they bore down harder when they suspected him of pulling strings to get a horse in a regiment like the Third Pennsylvania while old-timers grumbled around on foot. They said he was a personal friend of Ocean Pond, whom Sheridan valued more than his staff officers because of the way he cared for Rienzi. Several times Mike Sheridan had spoken to him. Once the general himself had pulled up to ask him how things were going. That was characteristic of both Sheridans, but jealous troopers made something of it.

Rick wanted to fight and he wanted to cry, but he did neither. He crammed his head with everything in the drill book that Ocean could explain to him, and he supplemented it with the wisdom of his own horse that he named Penn, for the regiment. Penn was an old cavalry mount and, if given free rein, would obey most commands and bugle calls.

"You're learning one big lesson," Ocean told Rick. "A man and his horse should be a team, not merely a rider and a horse. And they should be matched for brains. A fool man can ruin a good horse and a fool horse can cost a man his life. They must work together. Get that — work!"

"Gosh, we do work," Rick said. "We're so tired we don't hear taps. At least, I don't. Do you?"

"Always. It's the only sweet, gentle sound in war. Somebody should put up a monument to General Dan Butterfield, who made it up."

"How is Rienzi? I see him and the general going like a shooting star now and then."

"What a team they are!"

"I saw General Grant the other day. He's not much to look at — sort of stoop-shouldered, rode at a gallop and leaned forward as though he couldn't wait for his horse to get there."

"That's Grant," Ocean said. "He'll pass a whole regiment that way, yet every man will say later Grant looked him square in the eye. They say his eyesight is due to his diet; every day he eats a pound of butter broiled on a stick over a fire till it is crisp."

Rick did not laugh, for he was learning.

"What's up?" he asked. "You never talk silly unless you are worried."

"I'm not exactly worried." Ocean twisted his lips. "It's just that things are building up. Before long, maybe by the first of May, they'll burst wide open."

"Good!" Rick knocked his heels together. "Then I'll see some real action."

"I wouldn't be a mite surprised."

Rick had been in the service too short a time to appreciate what had happened to the Army of the Potomac since Grant and Sheridan took over. However, he learned from the veterans of the tightening up all along the line. For years thousands of officers and men had been enjoying soft jobs. From the War Department in Washington to remote posts the machine had been topheavy with brass. Every headquarters had been overstaffed, many an unimportant officer had his escort of cavalry and a dozen aides to fetch and carry for him. Inefficiency had soaked to the bottom of the pyramid and whether it was clerks or teamsters several had done only the work of one man. Drill had been lax, discipline and morale so low that thoughtful soldiers had dreaded the opening of the spring campaign.

Then Grant galloped out of the West. Change came

overnight. Disregarding politicians and favorite sons, he took the army by the collar and snapped it into line. Pomp and ceremony went out the window and incompetency was thrown after them. Always in motion, forever studying the faces of his men, the commander recognized ability and used it where it was needed, whether that was heading a division or driving mules.

The first jolt he gave the army, the country and the enemy was when he ordered General Sheridan to take all the cavalry and use it. Even President Lincoln at first regretted the choice of the young, undersized, hot-tempered officer who smoked a little meerschaum pipe and slept in his uniform.

Sheridan went to work, and so did every other cavalryman whether he liked it or not. Pretty officers found themselves without escorts and aides, troopers waiting for fresh mounts were told to quit loafing and start training as infantry, and fancy squadrons that had been ornamenting the streets of Washington were sent into the field in a hurry. Sheridan's idea, and he was supported by Grant, was to make the cavalry a single striking force capable of acting either with other branches or independently.

Rick picked up this information, and much more, during the first two weeks of April. Day after day, in churning mud and flying dust, he felt the quickening pulse of impending action. Hurry was the watchword and he threw in all he had to learn fast and well. With innumerable assists from Penn he mastered a passable amount of the rudiments of drill, grasped the proper way to handle his saber, seven-shot carbine and six-shooter. In the sham battles, when regiment after regiment, yelling and firing blanks, charged against ranks of infantry with fixed bayonets, he gathered a faint idea of the real thing. And because it was make-believe he thought it was glorious.

Two more weeks and it was the first of May. After the month of relentless drilling Rick felt hard and tough and imagined himself to be a veteran. This was war, said the boy who had never fired a shot. But he would soon. The tempo of preparation was rising by the hour. An immense concentration of troops was taking place on the Rapidan, the greenest recruit could see that much.

Grant was seen occasionally, always at a gallop, and Sheridan was everywhere, carrying his little black hat in his hand because it would not stay on his head. Rienzi came in caked with mud and lather, but never dejected. Ocean worked on him from the tips of his ears to the nails in his shoes, as though the war depended on it. Possibly it did, for after one short month every one of his ten thousand troopers had, in varying degrees, caught the spirit of Little Phil and accepted the tireless black horse as his symbol. To Rick the horse was a hero and to Ocean he was the glorified composite of all Morgans.

"I bet you'd rather have this job than a general's commission," Rick said one evening, as he watched Ocean rubbing Rienzi's shining flanks.

"Right."

"How come you haven't been promoted for taking care of him?"

"One reason people like horses is that horses never ask personal questions," Ocean answered, without missing a stroke of his brush.

"I'm sorry I was nosy." Rick turned away in embarrassment.

He walked to the edge of camp and watched a line of infantry slogging along in the fading light, already dog-tired but with miles yet to go. The last man in one file was Ed Potts. In spite of the uniform, there was no mistaking that stupid face, nor the voice when he whined aloud that he was too tuckered out to take another step.

"Shut up and keep goin'," a noncom barked. "You've been behind every day for a week. Was you born in a caboose?"

The ranks plodded on. Rick smiled at the way Ed was running true to form. Rick was glad they had finally gotten him. They would never meet again, he thought. This belief was something to be remembered as a regrettable error.

$$\star \ 7 \ \star$$

To RICK, THE EARLY PART OF THE THIRD OF MAY WAS ABOUT like other days — mess, roll call, drill. But as the hours passed an indefinable tightness permeated the air. General Grant rode past the drillground twice, going fast. Sheridan was frequently seen and his three aides, Mike, Captain James Forsyth and Lieutenant T. W. C. Moore, dashed back and forth in all directions with messages. In the distance infantry moved in endless lines and over toward the railroad white streams of baggage wagons flowed toward the river. Toward evening the troopers were issued live ammunition. This was it.

"What have you heard around headquarters, Ocean?" Rick asked, when evening mess was over.

"Nothing." Ocean raised one of Rienzi's feet and tapped the shoe with a hammer to make sure it was tight. "But I have seen what everyone has seen — the Army of the Potomac getting ready to cross the Rapidan."

"Will there be a fight?" Rick was breathless.

"Nothing is certain in this world." Ocean examined another shoe. "But if we are to judge the future by the past, when the Army of the Potomac meets the Army of Northern Virginia the result won't be a clambake."

"How many on both sides?"

"Clams or troops?"

"Troops, you looney."

"In round figures, two hundred thousand."

"It will be awful, Ocean!"

"Yes."

"Think of all their folks. Have you got a family, Ocean?"

"I had thirty-seven children, but one night after supper I knocked 'em all in the head because they tried to pry into my business."

"There I go again. I'll never learn." Rick walked away stiffly. He could not understand then that on this night before his first battle he needed unsympathetic treatment to keep him from softening up.

Because he realized so little of what was happening on that momentous evening, he was asleep at the usual time. Once during the night he heard a troop leaving camp or passing through, saddles creaking, bits jingling, shoes clicking on stones, men talking in low tones. The sounds faded out toward the river, but he was too sleepy to understand that the Rapidan was being crossed and the campaign had begun.

Reveille blasted him awake and as he crawled out of his tent he saw it was still dark. Someone struck a match, looked at a watch and grumbled it was three o'clock.

"What's the sense in getting up this early?" Rick muttered, pulling on his boots.

"We'll have to get up earlier than this if we want to get

the jump on Marse Robert," answered the man with the match.

"I'm sick of all this yammering about Lee."

"Wait till you've fit him three years like we have, whippersnapper."

"Shut up!" a noncom snapped. "Feed your horses. And see they're clean. We're not going in with straws in our tails."

When boots and saddles sounded at four o'clock it was light enough to see the companies forming. The whole world seemed alive with men and horses. Rick shivered and his hands felt damp on the bridle reins. He told Penn to take it easy, though his horse was much calmer than he. "Lead Out" the bugles sang, and the long lines began to move, the big flags and the little ones falling in at regular intervals.

It was a beautiful morning. Birds were singing in the blossoming dogwoods, celebrating the spring, unlike these men who had gone insane and were trying to kill and be killed at a time when life should be beginning. The cavalry trotted down the road between parked artillery and waiting infantry. The foot soldiers scorned the troopers and plastered them with insults, calling them "pillow pushers" and "butter legs." Offering fantastic rewards for a dead cavalryman. The horsemen retaliated with "froggers" and "mud eaters." There was much laughter and singing from those who had been in battle and knew what lay ahead.

The horses splashed into the river, where the roily water

looked golden in the early sunshine, and went on up a winding road into a gloomy forest.

"Here's the Wilderness, and the feller who named it
knew his business," said the trooper beside Rick. He was a
storekeeper from Michigan named Pike, with a saber scar
clear across his left cheek.

"You have been in it before?" Rick asked.

"I died in it twice — Chancellorsville and Fredericksburg.
It's no place to fight a battle, I tell you. The Old Man and
Bobby both know it, so we're going straight through this
time, thank the Lord."

"Don't be too sure what Lee will do," the man ahead
spoke up.

"He's no fool," Pike said confidently. "Wait till you
see this Wilderness — a hunk of hell about twelve miles
long and six wide, packed full of mud, scrub trees, mosquitoes and rattlesnakes. The Old Harry himself couldn't
get through it cross-lots."

"Any roads?" Rick asked.

"Two or three, as I remember. One of 'em is, or was,
partly planked."

"If it's only six miles we'll be out of it before noon."

"You poor fool!" said the man ahead. "Do you think a
hundred thousand men can be marched in half a day?"

"I didn't mean the whole army," Rick defended himself. "Just the cavalry under Sheridan."

"Sheridan's hands are tied," Pike said. "When I was
picketing last night I heard him and Meade jawing about

it. Meade still has the idea the cavalry's only fit to run errands."

"Meade's not top man," Rick remarked.

"He's next to it, and he has a lot to say."

"Meade's a good man," said the trooper in front. "A mite pompous mebbe, but honest as a church."

So they talked strategy, gossip and politics, as tens of thousands of soldiers were doing that morning, for the Union army was remarkably well informed. The horses plodded forward, attempting to switch off the flies that swarmed as the smell of sweat grew stronger. The forest was dark but not high, mostly scrub pine and dense under-growth so closely laced with vines that no one could see a hundred feet either side of the road. Small sluggish creeks crawled through the rotting vegetation, unblessed by a single ray of sunshine. There were a few tiny clearings, desolate, weed-grown patches surrounding solitary cabins of hewn logs.

Rick had supposed they would trot through the woods into open country and then go gaily about, looking for Rebels. But he had never seen an army move. The bulk of the troops was infantry, hundreds of regiments, with ar-tillery, baggage trains and ambulances. There were only three roads by which this huge mass could be funneled through the Wilderness. The first one, called the Orange Turnpike, ran east and west. Parallel to it, two or three miles south, was the Orange Plank Road. Crossing those two and running north and south by east was the Brock

Road. None of those highways were good and their only tributaries were lanes and paths that went nowhere. Under such conditions it seemed that only divine guidance could avert a perpetual traffic jam.

Daylight stretched full length across the dreary land. For Rick the world had contracted to his regiment, which spent most of its time waiting for no one knew what. "Give way to the right!" an officer shouted and General Grant galloped past. A few minutes later Sheridan followed, his face black as a thundercloud. In his wake, spurring to keep his own horse up with Rienzi, Mike gave Rick a grim look. Obviously, things were not going well.

The troopers argued and speculated and swore as they slapped flies and mosquitoes. If Little Phil had his way the cavalry would be going somewhere, not fiddling around in driblets all over the map. Probably Meade was holding things up. Why didn't Grant tell him who was running this army? The Old Man was boss, wasn't he? Perhaps, after all, he was no better than the other commanders, a mere tool of the War Department in Washington. Everyone knew the War Department didn't know enough to pour soup into a tin horn — and so on. At any rate, those soldiers were not awed by gold braid.

But they were awed by something else. As night approached they camped in a field by a ruined house called Wilderness Tavern. There the armies had fought the year before on the road to Chancellorsville. As they built their fires veterans talked in low tones about the comrades whose bones lay still unburied among the weeds. Rick clung fearfully to Penn as he groomed him in the eerie twilight and when taps sounded for the living and the dead, he was not the only one who shivered.

The bones remained, but the ghosts vanished at dawn. It promised to be a clear, hot day. The optimism usually associated with sunrise was held down close to earth by a blanket of apprehension. The men's thoughts moved under it, earthbound and unable to sense the sparkle of the blue sky. The toughest veterans remembered that the skeletons in the tall grass had been soldiers only a year ago, doing the hateful work of the moment in order to enjoy the blessings of the future. There had been men of valor on both sides, fiercely divided by ideas; they were one now.

Rick trembled as he saddled Penn and waited for orders. Infantry was coming out of the woods and forming along the Turnpike, facing west. A slender general with long black hair and a twisted-up mustache walked his horse over and spoke to young Captain Parker, who commanded Rick's company. The captain, who looked like a pink-faced schoolboy playing soldier, listened, saluted and led his men down the road at a trot.

"Where are we going?" Rick wondered aloud.

"Looks like a coon hunt," Pike answered, that being slang for scouting.

The road was straight between the trees and white against the green-black walls of the forest. They jogged up a little hill and the captain reined in. Standing in their stirrups, the troopers looked over the rise and saw a foot column advancing. It was a good distance away but near enough to show men peeling off into the woods on either side. They were the first Confederate troops Rick had ever seen and he was so fascinated he completely missed the significance of their being there.

Parker pivoted his horse and sang out eagerly, as though bringing good news, "Lieutenant Giles, ride back and tell General Warren the Johnnies are coming."

"Yes, sir!" Giles saluted, pulled out of line and straightened away down the road.

Parker led his troop at a walk and Rick tensed for the moment when they would charge, yelling, and waving their sabers as they had practised. Then they stopped altogether.

"What are we waiting for?" Rick whispered to Pike.

"Orders, you fool," the veteran snapped.

They arrived before Rick's ears stopped burning. General Warren galloped up and hard after him came two guns.

"Feel out the enemy, Captain," Warren ordered.

"Yes, sir!" Parker replied. And the Battle of the Wilderness was on.

In that terrain reconnoitering would have to be done on foot. When the Rebs sent in a few musketshots at long range, the captain ordered seven fast rounds from the carbines by way of token, and then dismounted his men, assigning one in four to hold the horses beside the road. As the other troopers melted into the woods the big guns cut loose, the noise muffled by the undergrowth.

"Keep contact!" Parker shouted and immediately disappeared.

So did the entire company. Contact in that jungle would have required a solid line of men elbow to elbow. Trees, brush, vines and ferns made a green sea in which men vanished more completely than in water, for there were no ripples afterward. It couldn't be that officers expected to handle troops in such a place. They had bumped into each other accidentally and after a few shots would back off into open country.

To Rick that was a cheering thought, a sort of reprieve, and he felt very brave as he burrowed into the green mass and told himself his first battle was about over. Shots were popping ahead and he fired a few times to show he was taking part. Then he went forward leisurely, less interested in the enemy than in finding a comrade to go along with, for in spite of the excitement it was a lonesome place to be in.

There was a difference in the firing now. Sounds mingled, as though the lines were close together. There were noises like heavy drops of water smacking down on the leaves. The recruits saw a sapling buckle two feet from the ground and topple against a tree as a musket roared near by.

Rick hugged the ground, trembling. It would be awful to be wounded and lie there helpless and alone. He crept toward denser cover, looked into a tiny clearing, and felt his scalp prickle with horror. Across a log was a human skeleton and between the ribs a rattlesnake raised its head. Rick yelled in terror and started shooting, emptying his carbine and six-shooter. The bones flew apart, the snake coiled, stopped a bullet and went writhing away. The boy leaned against a tree and vomited.

He yelled when he felt a hand on his shoulder, then nearly folded up with relief when he heard Pike ask casually, "How are things with you, O'Shay?"

"I've been sick." Rick reloaded his carbine shakily. "It was the water, maybe."

"Yeh." Pike grinned. "We all drink at that stream sooner or later. Nice place for a battle, isn't it?"

"Is it a real battle?"

"Begins to look so. By the sound, infantry's fanning out on both sides of the road. They'll catch up with us pretty soon."

"Then what will we do?"

"Go along with 'em, pretty likely."

"On foot? But we are cavalry."

"Listen, son, horses are to transport men to where they're needed most. Never mind how we get there, it's what we do that counts."

Rick knew Pike meant it. He had recently re-enlisted for three years. He was like Ocean Pond.

"I don't know what will happen to me when I get there," the boy said, in a burst of confidence. "I am scared now."

"So am I," Pike admitted cheerfully. "Everybody is when the music starts. In the end it doesn't amount to a hill of beans."

"I suppose not — in the end." Rick glanced at the bones in the clearing and shuddered.

There was never a battle like that one. Soldiers on both sides disappeared in the forest as water is absorbed by a sponge. They went on fighting — that is, shooting in the

direction of the enemy — though no one could see anyone. By the noise, reinforcements were being sent in and
after a few minutes wisps of powder smoke were wandering
aimlessly under the trees as though they too were lost. There
was the smell of wood smoke as flashes kindled dry leaves.
The old-timers were more uneasy about that than about
the bullets, and they had good reason.

It was assumed that the Union line had overtaken its
skirmishers, but there was no way of telling where the line
was. Individuals and groups pushed toward sounds, some of
them walking backward to force a way through the tangled
vines. That the Confederate strength was growing could be
told by the way the firing extended farther to right and left.
And it was increasingly nearer. Leaves and twigs fell
steadily and bullets thudded into tree trunks. Drums were
beating unintelligibly, confused in the echoing woods. The
impression got around that the Union line had been ordered
to halt and hold. Such commands had not actually been
given, but the idea hit everyone at about the same time:
lie low and let the Johnnies do the bushwhacking.

Smoke streamed through openings in the green wall,
settled in the heavy air, adding to the gloom and the inten-
sity of the flashes. Rick lay on his belly, too frightened to
move a finger. Bullets were clipping around him like busy
shears and there was no reason on earth why he should
escape. Then what? Another skeleton in the brush? He
broke under the strain and leaped into a clump of head-high
ferns, yelling and flailing with his saber. The blade whirled
from his hand as a musket roared. He whipped out his six-

shooter and shot at a face between the fern fronds. It pitched toward him and a man in butternut brown lay almost at his feet.

"Got me, Yank," the Confederate muttered.

"Why did you make me do it!" Rick sobbed.

The man did not answer and the ferns that had been trembling under his body were still.

"Get down!" Pike's voice was sharp beside Rick. "Don't stand there, you fool!"

"I killed him!" Rick began to tremble. "I'm going to get out of this."

Pike's fist shot out and Rick sprawled on the ground. "I told you to stay down, and I meant it."

Rick lay there, horrified at what he had done, yet so scared that when Pike crawled away he crawled with him. Reinforcements poured in, adding to the confusion. The woods were full of invisible men and the noise they made was everywhere so that no one could tell whether he was in front, behind or on the flank of the enemy. It was useless to try to face the firing because bullets were coming from all sides.

Companies formed in little clearings, tried to get their bearings and lost contact when they re-entered the jungle. More and more, men stumbled over other men dead or dying, Yanks and Rebels, facing in all directions. The smoke was so heavy that the green wall looked gray; it lay along the ground in banks like dirty snow or eddied and twisted in air currents. It was pungent wood smoke now and soldiers who could look up saw the treetops whipping in a high wind. Above the roar of battle rose the crackle of flames and human voices pitched to screams.

Rick was no longer afraid, his brain was too numb to register emotion. In the midst of two armies he was alone, completely lost, unable to retreat if he had wanted to because he did not know where the rear was. He lay in a hollow at the foot of a knoll, gripping his carbine with both hands. As the smoke billowed over him he twisted sideways and noticed a sort of tunnel winding off to the left — a cow path. It offered a way to go somewhere, and go fast, for flames were dancing on top of the knoll. Against their light two arms were waving wildly and a wounded man was probably screaming, though he could not be heard. Rick ran up the knoll, dropped his carbine and dragged the man back by the shoulders.

"Put your arms around my neck. I'll carry you piggyback," he yelled.

He knelt and, when the hands were locked across his chest, lifted the other, caught him under the knees. Rick went down the path and along it for seeming miles. Several times he saw men in the gloom, but kept on, determined to get this helpless soldier to a safe place. Bless the cows that had made that path!

A rush of comparatively pure air hit Rick and the smoke lifted. He glanced ahead and saw a road that looked unbelievably wide and smooth. Right there it was empty, though on either side he could see troops in the distance. He put his burden down and asked the man if he knew where they were.

"Ah cain't rightly say, suh," the other answered.

Rick eyed him sharply and found that under the dirt and smoke he was wearing a gray uniform much too large for him.

"You're only a kid, Johnny." Rick grinned at him.

"Suh," the boy's voice was absurdly dignified, "in Virginia we are men at fifteen."

"You don't look it." Rick glanced down the road. "I guess your friends are moving this way, so I'll get along. Got any water in your canteen?"

"No, suh."

"Here, take mine." Rick laid it beside him.

"Suh," the boy said, pale and helpless and proud, "Ah hate all Yankees, but you are a gentleman."

"Thank you, Johnny. Good luck!" Rick was away, keeping in the ditch.

He was immensely relieved to find himself out of the woods, amazed to learn he was unhurt and gratified to feel calm and free from that nightmarish fear. Not that there was any suggestion of tranquility anywhere. The road and ditches were strewn with dead or sorely wounded men in blue. Walking wounded were straggling toward the rear through a litter of dead horses, overturned artillery and every kind of discarded equipment.

"What happened?" Rick asked an artilleryman who sat on a caisson holding a bloody leg.

"Same old thing." The man ground his teeth. "This Ulysses Grant they talk about is only Useless Grant. What's going on in the woods?"

"I don't know. You can't see the length of your nose in there."

"Where are the ambulances? Why doesn't somebody help me?"

"I'll help you walk."

"I'm not going to walk. I've a right to an ambulance and I'm going to have one."

"Sure." Rick moved on. "If one doesn't show up within a week, write your Congressman."

Around a bend in the road he saw masses of infantry coming up, with horse artillery but no cavalry. A riderless horse nipped leaves from a dogwood and waited for someone to tell him what to do. Rick took over. As he settled in the saddle Lieutenant Mike Sheridan galloped up looking worried.

"Oh, it's you, O'Shay. Have you seen General Sheridan?"

"No, sir."

"Everywhere I go I just miss him. Perhaps we can corner him. Come back to the crossroads and turn left while I go right. If you find him tell him . . . No, wait, I'll write the message." He pulled out his notebook, scribbled in it and handed the folded sheet to Rick. "How is the fight going?"

"That is what I was wondering, sir."

"Lee is attacking — that's all I know."

They spurred away along the narrow strip between the advancing columns and the forest. Rick turned at the crossroads and saw some tents on a knoll in a clearing. In front of them General Grant sat on a stump, whittling a stick and smoking a cigar. Rick chose a young captain, who stood apart from a knot of higher officers, and saluted.

"I have been ordered to find General Sheridan, sir," he said. "Can you tell me where he is?"

"He went south a few minutes ago."

"Thank you, sir."

Rick finally found Sheridan superintending the building of log breastworks. The place was under fire and the wood smoke was heavy, but neither the general nor Rienzi seemed excited. "Wait for an answer," Sheridan said. He read the note and as he sat thinking about it he filled and lighted his little meerschaum pipe. Then he wrote a reply and handed it to Rick. "My compliments to General Grant."

"Yes, sir!" Rick saluted and wheeled.

"Hold on, O'Shay!" Sheridan thrust the pipe toward him. "I can't keep track of my aides. When you are at liberty report to me for messenger duty."

"Yes, sir!"

Thus Rick fell head over heels into luck, for to be an aide, even an unofficial one, to Little Phil was a promise of being on the spot when things happened. And they happened so fast the boy could not keep them in focus. That evening he heard from Ocean, who had a surprisingly clear understanding of news as it went through headquarters, that the battle losses had been heavy on both sides and nothing had been gained. Ocean also said Sheridan had refused to tie his cavalry down to the job of protecting Meade's baggage trains, saying he had more important work to do.

He did it next day when, without waiting for orders, he sailed in and stopped the Confederate cavalry under Jeb Stuart, who was on his way to attack the Federal rear. Meade was hopping mad, so Ocean learned. At the time he outranked Sheridan and, unless Grant ordered otherwise, would have the say-so about the cavalry. He commanded it to fall back and the little Irishman was obliged to obey, though he managed to concentrate his spraddling squadrons for the blow he expected.

It came that night, May sixth and seventh, after another awful day in the Wilderness. Stuart struck at what he supposed to be disorganized Union cavalry and was set back on his heels. Rick had his first sight of General Custer of the long golden curls and the devil's own knack for fighting.

Presently, so far as ordinary soldiers could make out, there was a change in Grant's plans. The senseless, almost stationary, woods fighting changed to movement. As Rick dashed back and forth with messages, half the time lost in the maze, he saw more and more troops jamming the road. He saw, too, that Sheridan's face was getting blacker. Bits of conversation pieced together indicated that Meade, who was an honest man and thought himself right, was blocking all of Sheridan's orders to use the cavalry in force, as the Confederates were doing.

It came to a head about noon. Sheridan galloped up to Meade's tent, angrily demanding to know why every order had been countermanded until the cavalry was helplessly confused. Meade, who was usually the aristocratic gentleman, also exploded, saying that the infantry was in a tangle because the cavalry clogged the roads. The heat increased until, in a final burst of fireworks, Sheridan roared that he could smash Jeb Stuart's cavalry if Meade would mind his own business, but as he would not, Meade could run the Cavalry Corps himself and Sheridan was through.

Those who listened gasped, for this was no picayune row. Things were bad enough anyway, but this might tear the army apart, for Sheridan was the idol of his troops and Meade had a fine record with the infantry. Both officers knew the danger, and Meade, perhaps thinking Grant would reprimand Sheridan, went over to the commander's tent and told him what had happened.

"He even boasted he could whip Stuart if I did not interfere," Meade sputtered, trying to recover his dignity.

"Did he say that?" Grant blew a long cloud of smoke from his cigar.

"Yes, sir, he did."

"Then," Grant said softly, "let him go and do it."

So, as Ocean later remarked to Rick, Little Phil could now show 'em what he was good for.

☆ 8 ☆

IN SPITE OF GRANT'S EFFORTS THE BATTLE ON THE WHOLE remained stationary. Troops were constantly on the move and yet they went nowhere in particular. There was no place for them to go except around and around in that awful, burning, roaring tangle. Officers tried to lead their men by compass, but no one could follow a straight line. Whole regiments sometimes managed to hang together and move into position, only to find they were far ahead or behind or to one side of where they should be.

There were innumerable fearful little battles within the big one, heroic charges, panicky retreats, hour after hour of steady slugging from behind the same logs and trees. Men on both sides were constantly blundering into each other and being made prisoner, to wander around together and perhaps join in a mutual fight against forest fires. Sometimes individuals or larger units declared impromptu truces to rescue the wounded from the flames, struggling to save those they had tried to kill five minutes before. When no rescuers were at hand the helpless men stopped screaming and took what seemed to them the only way out.

At night it was even worse. The armies did not back off

and rest, but lay where they were, for there was no desig-
nated place of respite, no way of knowing who held possession of the next knoll or clearing. Officers tried to throw out
pickets, but the men were jittery with fatigue and fired at
anything or nothing, making the shooting constant. A majority slept from exhaustion for an hour or two until the
creeping flames reached them. Then they stamped and
cursed and groaned and moved away to sleep again. In their
sleep they choked on the air that was heavy with the smell
of powder and wood smoke and burning flesh.

Now and then Rick realized in amazement that he was
still alive. The sound of whining bullets was everywhere
and twice he rode through showers of shrapnel and grape, a
message gripped between his teeth, one hand on the reins,
the other on his revolver. Sheridan and his aides went unscathed, though Mike and Forsyth each lost a horse. Rick
was still afraid — fear was always in the back of his mind —
but bullets were less to be feared than the possibility of be-
traying the trust the general had put in him. Every greenhorn wasn't fortunate enough to work personally with his
idolized commander.

Since the row with Meade, Sheridan had been working
furiously, pulling out his scattered cavalry and concentrating
it at a crossroads called Aldrich's Station, southeast of the
main Wilderness. While one crucial battle raged in the
forest, he had detached himself from it and was planning a
campaign of his own. He did not work it out slowly at a big
table covered with maps, but at top speed in the saddle. It
was as though he had two brains, one busy with staff work at

headquarters, the other noting every detail in the field. He even called troopers by name and asked if they were getting good food. He paid special attention to the horses. Were there plenty of horseshoe nails? Wash the cut in that bay's back so the flies won't blow it. Tie that one shorter so he can't get his foot over the rope and saw his leg.

"I honestly believe," Rick said, during one of those rare spells when he had time to talk with Ocean, "I honestly believe he has every man and every horse on his mind."

"That's what an officer is for," Ocean answered, brushing Rienzi's saddle blanket.

"But he has so many big things to think about."

"He has two pockets in his shirt, one for big things and one for small things. It's keeping them balanced that makes his shirt fit."

"How is Rienzi standing it?"

"As usual. Of course, I'm feeding him a special battle ration. It's exploded gunpowder ground fine and mixed with a wildcat's holler."

"You're worried or you wouldn't talk that way."

"That's as true as you're a foot high, Rick. If Sheridan doesn't lick Jeb Stuart, as he has promised to do, he may just as well hang up his fiddle and his bow. The soldier politicians in this army are giving him one chance, because Grant says so, but if that chance fails even Grant can't save him. Nor can Lincoln, if the politicians set out to down him. They hate independent Phil Sheridan, the pint-size son of an Irish laborer."

"You know a lot about things," Rick said admiringly.

"I know that for the first time we have a cavalry leader to match Stuart and Hampton and . . ." Ocean broke off suddenly and bent over Rienzi's feet.

"Pond!" A man in civilian clothes was coming toward him. "I haven't seen you in a coon's age. Where have you kept yourself?"

"Eh?" Ocean grunted.

"I've sat at too many board meetings in New York not to remember you. In fact, I am here to inspect army goods on a contract from our firm."

Ocean stood up awkwardly. His mouth, usually puckered tight, hung half open and his eyes had a stupid stare.

"I guess you've got the wrong pig by the ear," he said, in a rasping voice. "I don't set on no board. I'm a private in Ginral Grant's army 'n' I git thirteen dollars a month fer takin' care of hosses, not fer settin'."

"You must excuse me," the stranger said hastily. "As you stood with your back turned, the resemblance was striking."

"I'm the same feller, front side 'r back side." Ocean grinned foolishly.

"Obviously." The man continued to look at Ocean. "Can it be that you were injured in the war? The Pond I knew dropped out of sight suddenly."

"A mule stepped on my big toe 'most a year ago and it ain't well yit. I mean the toe, not the mule."

The stranger turned to Rick. "Do you know this man?"

"Yes, sir." Rick did not bat an eye. "He enlisted in Elmira, New York, two years ago."

"My mistake." The man took a cigar from his pocket and gave it to Ocean.

"Much obleeged, mister." The grin was wider. "Call ag'in when you're down this way."

He watched the stranger disappear, then said in his usual tone, "Thank you, boy."

"Don't mention it." Rick felt queer about the whole thing.

"I will sometime," Ocean promised, and resumed work on Rienzi.

The big black horse was saddled long before daylight next morning, May ninth. Sharply at six o'clock one of the most spectacular movements of the war began. Quietly, at a walk, General Sheridan rode onto Telegraph Road that reached from Fredericksburg to Richmond. For once his hat was on his head and, as usual when on horseback, he looked tall and powerful, though he was worn down to a hundred and fifteen pounds. His escort was with him, one carrying the red and white two-starred headquarters flag. Falling in behind, four abreast, was a solid column of nine thousand troopers, seven batteries of horse artillery and an ammunition train. The line was thirteen miles long. The men carried three days' rations and enough grain to feed their horses until evening.

Heretofore, Federal cavalry raids had been small affairs, pulled off at top speed and lasting until the horses were exhausted. Sheridan had always believed that nothing was gained and much was lost by whooping things up before a battle grew hot, thus wasting the energy of men and horses.

He was going out to look for Jeb Stuart and he wanted to save his breath for that business. He would need it, too, for the gay Confederate cavalier had never been outwitted, outridden or outfought by the Yankees.

"O'Shay!" the general called suddenly. "Find Ocean and tell him Rienzi is slobbering. He doesn't like this new bit. I want the old one."

Rick located Ocean a mile down the road, keeping his eye on the wagon that carried his portable blacksmith's forge.

"Do you want me to take it up to him?" Rick asked.

"No." Ocean took the bit carefully out of the wagon. "I want to make sure it sets easy."

Rick winked at the man next to him. "He and the general must have everything just so."

"It's about time," the soldier said vigorously. "There's been too much by-guess-and-by-gosh in this army."

"There sure has," Rick said, as though he had been in the service for years. A fellow wasn't a recruit after he had been in battle with General Sheridan and was riding right up front with him, even if the position was that of errand boy.

They were taking part in something new in cavalry raids. All that day the cavalry almost sauntered along, crossing the Ny, Po and Ta rivers with no trouble except one brush with enemy horsemen. The burning Wilderness had been left far behind and by night Sheridan was somewhat to the rear of Lee's army and heading for Richmond. Morale was so high that even brigadiers were betting they would take the Confederate capital, though the commander did not encourage such talk. He had faith in his men, but sincere respect for the ability of his opponents.

Toward evening two-thirds of the force camped on the north bank of the North Anna River, where they found ample grass and an atmosphere of incongruous tranquility. General Custer led his brigade across the stream to see what he could find at Beaver Dam Station and stumbled on a pleasant surprise. First the bright-haired boy, who was happiest in a yelling, shooting charge, nabbed a train loaded with about four hundred Yankee soldiers being taken to a Southern prison camp. Then he picked up and burned two more trains with a hundred carloads of food for Lee's army. While they were at it they ripped out ten miles of track and telegraph lines.

It was a token performance that, as Ocean explained to Rick, put Jeb Stuart between the devil and the deep blue sea. The audacity of Sheridan's move had the Rebel stumped for once. He could not guess whether the little man on the big horse was planning to strike at Richmond or the rear of Lee's army.

"What would you do if you were Stuart?" Rick asked.

"Shoot Rienzi." Ocean polished a buckle with moist sand.

"Be serious."

"I am serious, boy, as serious as seven deacons sitting on a graveyard fence. Lose Rienzi and Sheridan may fail. If he does, Grant may fail, and if he does — see what I mean?"

"You pretty near worship that horse."

"Only the Almighty is worthy to be worshipped," Ocean reproved. "When I realize how much depends on Rienzi these days I stand in awe of him."

"There are other good horses."

"Sure. But, as I've told you before, there is something mysterious about the origin of the first Morgan. Nobody knows who his ancestors were and there was never one like him before. All of a sudden this horse appeared, stronger, smarter, more courageous than any other horse. And his offspring are made of the same stuff. I tell you, boy, the Almighty created the breed so there would be one ready when Phil Sheridan needed a superhorse to save the Union. Think I'm a fool?"

"No. You may be right. What are you going to do after the war? Go round lecturing about Morgan horses?"

"After the war?" Ocean puckered his lips. "I have a plan that may interest you — after the war. Now go to bed so things can quiet down and Rienzi get some sleep."

The next day was still more amazing. The only Federals who showed any signs of hurry were the hundreds or so troopers that Sheridan had trained as his personal intelligence staff. They were disguised as farmers, peddlers, some even as Confederate soldiers. Since the start of the campaign they had been scouring the country for every scrap of information. And they had got it. By midday the general knew that Stuart was driving his splendid troops to the limit to block the road at the hamlet of Yellow Tavern, six miles from Richmond. Sheridan was happy about it as he rode leisurely up and down, smoking his pipe, talking with the men and keeping an eye on the horses. He had so much time on his hands that early in the afternoon he ordered camp made at a place where the grass and water were good. There, well into enemy territory, the raiders had a long, refreshing rest. While the whippoorwills called and the soldiers laughed and sang around the fires the war seemed far away.

It was not. Early in the morning Sheridan knew Stuart was at Yellow Tavern and was hurrying up all his strength to make a stand there. This was it. Now the general must make good his word to Grant or join the long list of those who had gone down before the gallant horseman in the plumed hat and crimson-lined cape.

Sheridan went into action with everything he had. One division, two, then a brigade of a third advanced at the double. The men were not whooping troopers now, but grim, dismounted fighters. The power of their repeating carbines was terrible. The Rebels were as good soldiers as ever lived, yet they were knocked back several hundred yards before fire from one of their batteries slowed the Union push.

Rick had started out close behind Mike, Forsyth and Moore. As things warmed up, the aides were sent on separate missions and Rick was left riding only a length from the general. There was no cover for him this time. He was up there, a beautiful target, trembling all over but urging his horse to keep up with Rienzi. The big charger was glorious, a battle demon to look at but sensitive to his master's touch on the reins. Sheridan was in his glory, not melodramatically, but furiously intent on straightening his lines, galloping back and forth, roaring orders, waving his little black hat. Rick thought, with all those bullets in the air they'll hit him. They'll get me too. It would be easy to fall back and dismount and hug the ground. He didn't order me to stay with him — but I'm staying.

"O'Shay!" He heard Sheridan's voice above the tumult and saw the big horse pivot.

"Yes, sir!" Rick was beside him.

"There's no time to write an order." The general's mouth was close to Rick's ear and his eyes were blazing. "Custer's brigade is back in reserve. Tell him to hit the enemy's left, hell for leather."

"Yes, sir!" There was nothing to be afraid of now. Sheridan had expected him to be there when needed and he had not failed.

Custer was the man for the job. With saber high, long yellow hair flying, he led his regiments full tilt into the fight. They went clear through the enemy line, cut down the crews of three batteries and sent the Rebels reeling. Blue and Gray, mounted and on foot, met and mixed in a terrific hand-to-hand battle that was made up of hundreds of little slashing, shooting fights. Sheridan was in the thick of it and Rienzi, teeth bared and eyes flashing, appeared to need no guidance. Jeb Stuart was there, graceful and handsome as he stood in his stirrups trying desperately to rally his men. Troopers on both sides milled around him, slashing, shooting, trying to ride each other down. Suddenly Stuart swayed and clutched his saddle. An aide caught him in his arms, and another held their two horses together. With a gesture, which was a tribute to his honor, the Blue riders reined back and allowed the Gray horsemen to carry their commander away from his last battlefield.

Rick reloaded his revolver and bored into the fight to be near Sheridan. Two Rebels swung toward him. He felt one's saber fan his face; the other would have caught him across the neck if his own horse had not plunged ahead and gone down in a heap. Rick landed on his hands and knees and came up in a whirlpool of plunging horses. A hand grabbed his collar and he was snapped off his feet, coming down behind the saddle of a Blue rider. They crashed through a ring of fighters into a comparatively open space, and the man yelled over his shoulder, "Get yourself a horse!"

The voice was familiar and Rick stared at the back of Ocean Pond. He was bareheaded, his gray hair stuck straight up and his revolver was poised at a rakish angle.

"You're supposed to stay with the wagons," Rick shouted stupidly, he was so surprised to see Ocean in battle.

"Shut up and get a horse," Ocean roared. "I can't wait around all day for you."

There were dozens of riderless horses, some terrified, others calm with the wisdom of old campaigners. Rick caught one and rode back into the fight. He had no idea how long it lasted. Stuart's line was broken, but another Rebel leader, whom he later learned was General Gordon, brought in fresh troops and threatened to turn the tide. Then he too was shot down and his men lost heart.

By late afternoon the Confederates were in full retreat. Sheridan had smashed their boasted cavalry, the pride and glory of the South. He might well have called it a day, but he would not rest. He led his men through the outer defenses of Richmond. He sat on his horse, looking at the city and listening to the alarm bells. It was a prize that the North had coveted since the first day of the war and he was tempted as never before.

"I can take it if I want to," he said to Mike.

"You'll be a hero if you do, Phil." His brother's tone was eager.

"But I couldn't hold it. The Rebels would swarm in from all directions and drive me out."

"Still, you would be the one who captured Richmond. Your name would ring around the world."

"Yes." Sheridan twisted his hat in his hands. "But that selfish fame would cost the lives of a thousand of my boys. No, Mike, I can't afford it."

He turned Rienzi from the city and galloped toward the Chickahominy crossing. It was enough for him to have kept his promise to Grant.

☆ 9 ☆

AFTER THE RAID RICK FELT RATHER COCKY. IT WAS A NEAT piece of work and he was proud of his small part in it. Grant was gratified with the material result and, more, with the proof that at last he had found a subordinate with the intelligence and drive so dismally lacking in many Union officers of high rank. Even Meade, always a square shooter, congratulated Sheridan personally and praised him in dispatches. The rank and file worshipped him.

It seemed to Rick that he himself had won a great victory. Surely the recruit who had been terrified in the Wilderness had emerged from Yellow Tavern a hardened trooper. He had not known the heartbreak of the past three years and now, because the clouds had parted for a few hours, he thought the war was about over.

As he rode back to the Army of the Potomac he was drunk with glory. He saw tens of thousands of men who had survived the Wilderness, but he did not grasp the significance of what he saw. In the eyes of those dirty and tattered young men was something that would never be young again. Rick watched the endless string of ambulances without comprehending the freight of present and future agony they carried. He thought, though not too deeply, of the other army that lay forever where it had fallen in the battle that was never won or lost, and of Jeb Stuart, who was dead. Because he had gone unscathed through two battles, Rick believed he was as rough and tough as they come.

But he had no illusions about being weary. Since crossing the Rapidan two weeks before, no Yank had known a full night's sleep or had had his clothes off. The food, though sufficient, was usually awful by the time the men had it, undercooked or overcooked. Without coffee they might not have pulled through. There was plenty of it and they drank it everywhere at all times. Even in battle, if a soldier had water, he would take time out to kindle a fire under his tin cup. Rebels came through the lines and surrendered, after being promised all the coffee they could drink.

"Hurry up and boil," Rick said impatiently, as they stirred coffee in a dipper at the camp at Hayall's Landing on the James River. He laughed. "That sounds like Sheridan's 'Hurry up, hurry up, hurry up!' I've heard him say that a hundred times the past few days."

Ocean sat looking into the twilight. His blue eyes were as sharp as ever but there were tired wrinkles in his face and his mouth was puckered more askew. His companion wondered how a man of fifty-four could stand the pace and why he wanted to stand it.

"The best coffee I ever drank was flavored with doughnut holes," Ocean said slowly.

"Now what are you worrying about?" Rick asked. "Can't you spend a few minutes dancing on Jeb Stuart's grave?"

"Stop!" Ocean's eyes blazed. "Stuart was my friend."

"You have a lot of Rebel friends, don't you?"

"Yes."

"Which side are you on, anyway?"

"Don't be a fool, Rick." Ocean poured a cup of coffee with a steady hand. "War doesn't necessarily end friendship."

"You hate a man if you fight him, don't you?"

"Of course not. But if this war doesn't end soon it will brutalize us and we will all hate each other for generations to come."

"That can't be helped."

"It must be helped. It must stop before that happens. Right now we are callous beyond anything we imagined a few years ago. A few more years of it and we will be brutes. That's what worries me, son, not only the war but the effects of it."

"Shucks!" Rick shrugged and filled his cup. "You talk like one of those scholars I never could understand. Me, I'm just a plain soldier." He swaggered as he said it. "The war won't last long now we've got the Johnnies on the run."

"Did you read the newspapers that came in this afternoon?" Ocean took a few swallows from his cup. "Our General Sigel is running away from the Rebs as usual, this time in the Shenandoah Valley. Banks, a born fool, has failed in the Red River campaign. Ben Butler, a windbag, is cooped up at City Point. Sherman is barely moving toward Atlanta. Morale is so low in the North that the Copperheads may win their fight to end the war without victory." He emptied his cup.

"So," Rick said defiantly, "you're trying to tell me that, in spite of Grant and Sheridan, things are pretty bad. I don't believe it."

"I'm not trying to tell you anything," Ocean answered. "I'm asking you to think." He got up and walked away.

If Rick or anyone else in that army expected to be given time to think or recuperate, he was mistaken. Old soldiers recalled that after a battle there had always been weeks or months of rest and reorganization, but there was none of that now. The men needed it, for they were dog-tired and every unit was shot to pieces. Brigades were reduced to regiments, regiments to companies and some companies did not have a man to answer roll call. But Grant was not resting. His objective was to destroy Lee's army, something that could not be done by sitting down and waiting.

The Union army was the most democratic military outfit on earth. For that reason it was well posted on what it was doing and why. When the army began moving southeast out of the Wilderness the littlest drummer boy understood it was heading into open country to get around Lee. But Lee moved just as fast, and whenever the Yanks tried to outflank him he was always squarely in front of them. Generals had come and gone but neither side had ever lost confidence in Marse Robert.

It was a grim race. The armies marched parallel to each other and so close there was an almost continuous fringe of fire along the inner edges. Sheridan's job was now twofold, to lead the advance on the left and to keep the enemy cavalry too busy to start anything of its own. That meant that by day and by night the Yankee troopers were patrolling, jabbing and engaging in innumerable small fights that might become full-sized battles at any moment.

The men rested, if at all, in relays. They slept so soundly they didn't hear the firing unless it came from Union carbines; then they would be up instantly. If they happened to be near an infantry bivouac, they didn't hear the long roll of the drums at reveille and slept until the cavalry bugles sounded. It seemed incredible that they could endure so much and, for the most part, remain in good spirits. They sang and joked and sometimes when a handful of them met a few of the enemy, and officers were not present, they exchanged banter and Yankee coffee for Rebel tobacco. A few minutes later it might be necessary to hold a ford or take a bridge and the same men would kill each other. That they could do this as a matter of course was evidence of what Ocean had mentioned. Rick thought about it more and more, though he posed as a hard-boiled trooper.

Because he was young and had seen so much since leaving the farm, he could not take a steady view of anything. His position as unofficial aide to Sheridan left him unclassified as a soldier, yet he was forever in action. The general was indifferent to the fact that he was using a green private to carry messages for him. Mike was now a captain, as were the other aides, Forsyth and Moore, but this made no difference in their relations with Rick. They liked the boy and found him dependable. The overworked aides were glad of help.

A message might reach Sheridan in the middle of a stream, where he had borrowed a carbine and was fighting off an enemy patrol, or on a back road that he was exploring to see for himself how the land lay. He begged lights for his little pipe from soldiers' campfires and from General Grant's cigar. His uniform was so dusty and worn that a stranger would not have guessed the little man was anyone of importance. The men yelled at him when he passed, and he waved his hat in friendly fashion. They also cheered Grant, another little man in a rumpled uniform, riding hard, seldom speaking, seeing everything, working relentlessly to end the war he hated. They knew he hated it, that Lee hated it, that Lincoln hated it, that everyone hated it, and they asked one another, Why do we go on fighting? They could not quite answer that question, so they tried harder than ever to kill more and stop the killing.

The two armies drove ahead neck and neck, in sweltering heat and choking dust that changed the green fields to gray and made the sun a red balloon. Grant was trying to get ahead and turn the enemy's flank, but Lee matched him mile for mile. A swing of twenty miles would be brought up short less than five miles from where it started. Try as he might, Sheridan, in the vanguard, always found Southern horsemen between him and the road to Richmond.

There were long night marches, with little rest between. Nerves were jumpy and someone was always shooting or blundering into camp and starting false alarms. The men fell out by thousands, not because they wanted to but because they could not put one foot before the other. It was late May and for three weeks there had not been a day's letup. The cavalry had had it bad enough, but it had been worse for the other branches. While the horsemen were raiding, the artillery and infantry had endured the last of the Wilderness and then the horror of Spottsylvania. Still there was no rest nor prospect of rest.

As Rick rode back and forth he noticed that the country looked prosperous. The fields were clean; there were herds of dairy cattle; buildings were in good repair, for war had not come that way before. There was little pillaging, except for firewood, and people appreciated this, for they had been told they would be stripped of everything. Jubilant Negroes followed the army singing and dancing, innocently confident that their troubles were over.

Being a farmer, Rick winced when he saw the fields in their soft spring beauty gashed by miles of trenches. Both armies had learned to dig in, even if they intended to move on in a few hours. Tired as they were, when they made camp their first thought was to protect themselves and they started digging with bayonets and knives, before the wagons had time to bring up axes and shovels. They kept on digging until they had enough earth in front of them to stop a bullet.

The mail finally caught up with the army and the troops forgot their surroundings as they scrambled over to the military postman, hoping for news from home. They read letters as they plowed through the dust, lay in the trenches or sat by the campfires. Sometimes they laughed aloud and sometimes they wept. Sometimes they just sat thinking. Intimate details were discussed by buddies, whether they had been neighbors in the North or lived a thousand miles apart. Bivouacking together had given them mutual interests. Such friendships were sacred and if campmates were nosy or insolent to one, the other was always there to back him up. Plenty of fist fights started when the mail came, because of indiscreet remarks about someone or something back home. The boys were united in their will to fight the Johnnies, but Johnnies became secondary targets when anyone suggested that another fellow's sweetheart or church steeple or native town was not the finest on earth.

Rick had no trouble because his past had been nothing to brag about, and there was no mail of any kind in his present until one afternoon when he and Captain Sheridan were sprawled in the shade at headquarters waiting for the general to write dispatches. A battery opened up a mile across the river and a cannon ball plowed a furrow near by. Rick rolled over behind a tree and Mike ducked into the open tent.

"Phil," he cried, "you had better get out of here. They've got our range."

Sheridan looked up from the table. "Mike," he said placidly, "our mother taught us to keep the door shut in fly time. Please do so." He went on writing.

A few more balls came over and then the battery was silent.

"A letter for Rickert O'Shay!" a voice bawled. "Where is Private O'Shay?"

"Here." Rick stuck his head around the tree trunk and saw one of the military postmen. "Why don't you lie low for a minute?"

"The United States mail has the right of way," the man answered and tossed him a letter.

It was from Judge Meader. Rick read the signature first and got a warm thrill to know that he, like other soldiers had heard from home. It was a short letter, for the judge regularly wrote to dozens of boys at the front, but it was newsy and vigorous and personal. Ed Potts, said the judge, had been drafted two months ago. Rick knew that, for he had seen Ed the day before they crossed the Rapidan. He would thank the judge for all the news when he had time and could find a piece of paper.

Time, however, was full of action, every minute of it. Never for an instant did Grant let up, and Sheridan led the way. His horses were wearing out and he received fifteen hundred replacements, but no one suggested that the troopers might fold up. The commander issued repeated orders to press the advance and his chief of cavalry passed them down the line in two words: "Hurry up!" The men cheered, for at last they were getting somewhere. Movement was what they had long wanted and now that they were getting it their spirits were high.

Not that they were in a picnic mood, for always just across the Chickahominy River the Confederates were waiting for them. As the armies moved east and south Lee was being pushed into a corner, closer and closer to Richmond, until finally the capital was only five miles away. Lee decided he must hold the road at Cold Harbor. It was a desolate place, a tumbledown tavern surrounded by wide parched fields, slashed by gullies that angled southwest toward low hills. But it was a strategic crossroads, the place where a battle must be fought.

Grant knew it and sent Sheridan galloping away through dust so dense that its weight broke the roadside bushes. But Lee was there, his cavalry dismounted and dug in beside regiments of infantry. The Yankees also left their saddles. They crawled up close before they cut loose with their deadly repeating carbines. Armed only with smooth bores and single-shot rifles, the Southerners could not take it and retreated. The Blue horsemen entrenched furiously, knowing they would be lucky to hold what they had gained. Toward evening Lee threw in fresh infantry and the weary troopers pumped their guns for dear life and hung on by their eyelids.

In the darkness Rick bumped into someone who swore and called him a deserter.

"Oh, shut up!" Rick growled. "I'm too tired to desert if I wanted to."

"That you, O'Shay?" The tone changed.

"Yes. Who are you?"

"Captain Mike Sheridan. I'm sorry. I thought it was someone falling out."

"That's all right, sir. I can't find the general. Ocean says he handed over Rienzi without a word and disappeared."

"He is spending the night in the lines. The boys need his support. He told Grant he didn't think he could hold on.

Grant told him he must till the infantry comes up. The whole line will cave in if we give ground. Get some sleep, O'Shay. I shall stay with my brother and call you if he needs you."

"Thank you, sir. I'll be with Ocean and Rienzi."

The first of the infantry, the Sixth Corps, arrived in the morning. It had marched all night through such a cloud of dust that the men were half-blind and strangled. They formed their battle line in support of Sheridan and dropped where they stood, too used up even to boil coffee. Fortunately the enemy was waiting for its own reinforcements and was not pressing the attack.

In spite of the lull, Sheridan knew a crisis was at hand. More troops must be found and he sent his aides pounding back and forth commanding and imploring: "Hurry up! Hurry up! Hurry up!" The imperturbable Grant was showing signs of nervousness, and even Meade, who usually took his time, was cursing the delay. Reinforcements were on the way, but not fast enough. They were led by good men: Warren, Wright, Smith, Hancock, among others. All were trying to hurry and each kept getting in the way of the others. All day there were traffic jams, marches in the wrong direction and countermarches. The dust over the barren fields was a solid cloud that gritted between men's teeth, and the sun went down a dim red ball.

Before darkness the Sixth and Eighteenth Corps attacked along the road that led through the fields from Cold Harbor toward Richmond. If that road could be taken, if the Confederate army could be driven across the Chickahominy, if

Richmond could be captured, the war might end the next day.

The two corps charged the enemy trenches and in the twilight a long line of blinding fire met them at close range. The Federals faltered, then went forward. It was bayonet to bayonet, hand to hand. Men threw away their guns and pounded each other with their fists. Officers dismounted, picked up fallen muskets and clubbed their way ahead. The Rebels broke and in the near-darkness the warwise Yankees dug in where they were rather than risk a fight they could not see. They had done pretty well. The loss was heavy, but they had knocked out perhaps as many Johnnies, as well as taking seven hundred prisoners.

On the actual front things weren't going too badly and Grant ordered an all-out attack for dawn, when the lagging divisions should be in line. But as the night wore on everyone connected with operations knew the tangle was worse than ever. In the hot, dusty darkness the men might as well have been blindfolded. Soldiers, horses, guns and wagons were snarled in all directions, completely lost, unable to move, unable to camp, groggy with fatigue. Those who showed up at daybreak were little better than a mob, and that they were there at all was a tribute to their courage. To dream of fighting in that condition was out of the question, so the attack was postponed until four in the afternoon.

"How are things?" Rick panted, as he pulled up where Ocean was tightening one of Rienzi's shoes.

"Wonderful." Ocean twisted his dust-stained, unshaven face.

There was reason for worry. Grant's plans were sound and he was trying everything to make them work, but things would not straighten out. More than a third of Smith's men had fallen out during the night because they simply could go no farther without rest. The corps of Burnside and Warren were all mixed up and spent hours of weary marching trying to get where they belonged. Meanwhile the Confederates were feinting all along the line looking for a soft spot, while they dug miles of trenches. Those earthworks were what the Yankees worried about most.

By afternoon Grant saw that an attack that day would be foolhardy. He knew the delay had dulled the cutting edge of his blow, but there was nothing he could do about it. He set the hour for dawn the next day, June third. That was when it came — a bright morning after a night of rain and hail. The light was still dim when a lone signal cannon boomed. Seconds later the artillery and small arms were blazing from end to end of the three-mile front.

Sheridan had sent Rick with a message to Custer and the boy was returning when it began. After that he saw very little that happened. No soldier sees much of a battle except his own part in it. But Rick heard noise that surpassed all the noises he had ever heard if they had been rolled into one. It was a steady, savage thunder that spread over the field like a physical force so that men unconsciously braced against it. After a while he identified separate sounds that were more ominous because they were close at hand: the zip of one kind of bullet, the wail of another and the terrifying scream of shells.

"Get down flat!" a voice yelled in his ear and he saw Ocean pulling him from his saddle.

"I must stay with the general — if I can find him."

Rick bent over and as he did so his horse reared, swayed on his hind legs and fell broadside. Rick jumped free and flattened himself beside Ocean.

"War is awful on horses!" Ocean shouted.

"Did you ever hear anything like this?"

"No."

"I've got to find another horse."

"Stay where you are, you fool! Didn't you see the officers dismount and send their horses back at the last minute? Keep your head down till this lets up. It can't last long."

They would learn that where they were it lasted less than ten minutes. In some places it was half an hour. Then a series of heroic, desperate charges and the Union line was broken. Seven thousand Northerners lay on the field and hardly a Southerner was scratched. It was the worst blunder of Grant's life, perhaps of the whole war, and he was shaken as never before. The two days' delay was not his fault, but he had made the final decision to attack and he took full blame for the failure.

He also took full responsibility for continuing the campaign. He knew it must go on, whatever the cost. The men in the ranks shared his determination in a way that touched his heart. Despite its awful beating, his army did not retreat. With one accord the men pulled back a little, often not more than fifty yards, and stayed there, fighting. Covered by artillery, they lay flat, shooting back and scooping shallow trenches. Food, water, ammunition and orders were inched forward under a curtain of lead and iron. There was no way to relieve the wounded.

The battle roared all day and at night there was no rest for the men. They must dig their trenches deeper in order to live tomorrow. In the morning both sides were practically out of sight, and the guns opened up again. Another day, another night. More days and more nights, though few of the soldiers remembered how long they had been at it. Most of them had not had a full night's rest since they entered the Wilderness weeks before. They were indescribably dirty and ragged, but they were too groggy to care. They stood in the breathless trenches under the blazing sun, firing at nothing in particular like men in an endless dream, and caring less about enemy bullets than about their own thirst, for there was never enough water.

Rick fared better than most because Sheridan kept him on the move. The little general's face was grim with worry and drawn by the sympathy he felt for the men. Taut as a bowstring, he sent Rienzi galloping up and down, occasionally leaping from the saddle to enter the trenches, where his black hat bobbed around below the parapet.

"O'Shay," he said one afternoon as he stamped toward the tent, "you are dismissed for three hours. Get some rest."

"Thank you, sir."

"By the way, I have recommended you for a lieutenancy." He disappeared inside while Rick was thanking him.

Rick's weariness lifted as he sat there thinking. It was his first promotion and to receive it directly from the general was a double honor. It was better to have it come that way, man to man, than to be paraded before a whole regiment and be praised by a stranger. He wanted to whoop, but that gloomy field was no place for a celebration. Among thousands of dead and dying one man's happy shout, small as it was, would be heartless.

He wanted to get away as far as possible for a little while, so he rode slowly down a ravine where a Union mortar battery was lobbing shells over a knoll. Once there had been a grove on the top but it had been riddled by shellfire until only two trees were left. They were not more than three feet apart and he noticed with a start that a man was tied between them, facing the battery. He was directly exposed to firing from both sides and was bound to be hit sooner or later.

"What's the idea in that?" Rick demanded sharply of an artilleryman.

"Well," the soldier squatted on his heels, "he deserves to be shot, but he ain't worth wasting our ammunition on. The Johnnies will do it for us in time."

"That sounds pretty raw. What has he done?"

"Well, first-off he was under a wagon day 'n' night. Then he got brave enough to start robbin' corpses and wounded. We caught up with him only an hour ago. It's real fun to watch such a feller git what's comin' to him."

For no good reason Rick rode to the foot of the knoll and looked up at the prisoner. He looked again and stopped his horse. Though Ed Potts' face was twisted by fear, there was no mistaking it.

"Rick! Rick, cut me loose! They'll shoot me dead, they will!" His voice was a shriek. "Help me, Rick!"

"What did you ever do to help anyone?" Rick asked coldly, as sight of that hateful, stupid face brought everything back.

"Arrest me, put me in jail, put me anywheres, but git me outen here."

Rick rode away.

Dog-tired though he was, Rick could not sleep. Twilight crept over the field and still he lay awake in his dog tent. He had less regard for Ed than ever, but that was not what bothered him. The trouble was, he could not forget what Ocean had said about the brutalizing effect of war. It was true. Three months ago he would have fought to prevent anyone from torturing Ed, much as he disliked him. Punishment was one thing, but torture was abhorrent. Or it used to be that way. Now it was different, now war made crime pardonable. As Ocean had said, if it went on much longer no one would know right from wrong. If a fellow was to preserve his sense of values he must fight this brutalizing process with more determination than he fought his country's enemies. And he, Rick O'Shay, must begin right now by going back there and releasing Ed, if he still lived, and turning him over to the provost guard. That was the only honorable way to handle it.

When he crawled up the hill in the darkness Ed had disappeared

☆ 10 ☆

THERE WAS NOTHING RICK COULD DO. WHETHER ED HAD escaped or been killed, he was gone. On both sides there were skulkers like Ed and the men who stood up and did the fighting were sick and tired of them. Rick stopped worrying his conscience about the incident and went back to work.

There was plenty of work for everyone in that army. General Grant was heartsick over the failure at Cold Harbor, but he chewed his cigar and said nothing. That was his way. Hot-tempered officers found relief in profanity, but he used his steam to generate power. He had been commissioned to win the war and he knew the only way was to keep fighting. Intensely sensitive for all his rough exterior, he suffered agonies because his orders caused suffering and death. The soldiers, always quick to notice little things, saw that his shoulders stooped more, but there was a strength in the man. They had a growing faith that he could carry the load. So the troops cheered when he went among them and, while Northern civilians bitterly called him "the Butcher," the men with him were ready to stake their lives on his next move.

That move was made so quickly that for once even General Lee did not anticipate it. The idea was to slide the Union army out of the trenches at Cold Harbor and into the city of Petersburg, which was about twenty miles south of Richmond. It was a railroad center through which nearly all of Lee's supplies passed and if it could be captured the capital would fall quickly. If it were lost Lee would be starved out and forced to fight in the open. Part of Sheridan's troopers were to screen Grant's movements from the Confederates while others would keep the Gray cavalry busy by raiding the Virginia Central Railroad on which Lee depended for supplies from the Shenandoah Valley.

The battle of Cold Harbor was still going on when Mike Sheridan told Ocean to get his traps together and be ready to move.

"What's up?" Rick asked, as he helped Ocean load the portable forge on a wagon.

"One of two things." Ocean packed the bellows tenderly. "Either we are going to be sent to the Sahara Desert to fish through the ice or we are going to cut loose and pester the Johnnies."

"Any place is better than where we are," Rick said bitterly. "Do you know the dead aren't buried yet?"

"Do I know it? Where do you think I've been lately?"

"You haven't been all over the place forty times a day as I have. If the general expects me to keep up with him I wish he would give me a horse like Rienzi."

"Like him!" Ocean snorted. "There never was or never will be one like him."

"Not even Justin Morgan?"

"Not even him or General Lee's Traveler."

"Do you know the Rebel's horses too?"

"I am interested in horses."

"Sometimes you act mighty interested in Rebs."

"You are an amusing lad." Ocean twisted his mouth slowly. "In spite of your lack of manners, I hope you live to grow up. When the war is over I'll tell you why." He went on packing the wagon.

Soon after that, Sheridan's First and Second Divisions, some six thousand men, concentrated at Newcastle Ferry. It was to be a raid all right, for each rider carried forty rounds of ammunition, three days' rations and tied to his saddle two days' supply of grain for his horse. There were a few wagons for extra cartridges and miscellaneous necessities, and eight ambulances. The whole outfit was worn and weary, but there was no more grumbling than usual. If Phil Sheridan could take it, they could.

Once they were under motion, word filtered down that they were going to rip up the railroad near Charlottesville. There they would be joined by some cavalry from West Virginia and a small army under General Hunter, who had been wandering around in the Shenandoah Valley. The men cursed their luck, for they had no use for old Hunter. They would have less.

Two days later things began happening around Trevilian Station, where Sheridan and Custer on one side and Wade Hampton and Fitz Lee on the other met with all the slash and fury of traditional cavalrymen. For the next forty-eight hours Rick was one of a swirling, crashing, yelling, shooting mass of horsemen. Guns were taken and retaken, prisoners were captured, freed and captured again. Custer smashed Hampton, then Hampton smashed Custer. No one knew exactly what had taken place. In the end was the battle won or lost? No one seemed to know.

Sheridan's losses were heavier than at Yellow Tavern, but he hung on, waiting for Hunter to join him. However, Hunter was not the joining kind. Because of stupidity or cowardice, he disobeyed Grant's orders to the letter and marched off into the West Virginia mountains, where he was of no earthly use to anyone on the Union side. The Yankee troopers knew what they thought of him, but all they could do was retreat, for their ammunition was running out. Sheridan tore up a long stretch of railroad, collected four hundred wounded and five hundred prisoners, and went back to the Army of the Potomac, which by then was besieging Petersburg.

After those seven weeks of strenuous campaigning, Sheridan knew his men and horses must have rest. He had tried his troops under all conditions and found them good. They, in turn, had found an ideal commander and were willing to follow him anywhere.

Rick had never known such exhaustion as on the last day of the march to the rest camp at White House Point. If he could just lie down beside the road! But he hated stragglers, so he kept on, letting his horse follow the others. By midday it didn't matter much to him where they went. They would never get anywhere, just ride on and on until they died in the saddle. The thought of death did not alarm him. During the past week it had been his companion, even a good friend to some men he had seen. At present it was being alive that bothered him, the pain in every muscle and the hopeless mental depression. The only good thing was water; he emptied his canteen time after time and was always thirsty.

He was vaguely aware that Sheridan was up and down the line as usual. The general's face was black with disappointment at being obliged to retreat, and blacker still when he thought of General Hunter. Rick heard the men talking about it way off in the distance and they said there would be fireworks sooner or later. . . . They were here now. The sky was full of dancing bright spots. Then blackness, in which the man on his left bumped into him.

Rick felt cold and sick and wet with sweat.

"Hook his arm through his bridle rein so his horse won't run away," said a voice.

"Seems like somebody should stay with him," said another.

"What you think this is, an army or an old ladies' home?"

"But the bummers. You know how they sneak up at night to rob and murder a feller who's down."

"I know. Both sides ought to get together and hang a few of 'em. Well, come on."

"Wait a minute. Captain, ain't there a place in an ambulance for this feller?"

"There's not room for a sheet of paper. We have left twenty men already. Fall in!"

The line clattered on endlessly, and the dust rolled over Rick as he lay by the roadside. Not much of a place for a nap, he thought. He would be there only a few minutes, just until he got rested. That wouldn't be straggling. A fellow had to sleep now and then, even in wartime . . . A fellow had to sleep . . .

Rattledy-bang! He dreamed the kitchen stove had fallen down and Ed Potts was cussing him out for it.

"You'll get the devil for dumping that forge out 'side the road," said a voice that was not Ed's.

"There are other forges." That voice was familiar. "Wait till I spread this blanket, then give me a hand with him. Your blanket too."

"Here you be. This feller must be a friend of yourn."

"A cousin. His father was Uncle Wilbur Hawkins. Peg leg and red nose. Ever know him?"

"Can't say so."

"Fine old gentleman. So pious he shuddered every time he took a drink of rum — and how he loved to shudder! Now help me with this soldier."

"I don't need any help, Ocean," Rick muttered, and fainted.

Because the wagon was springless and the road had been worn out years before, Rick formed the hazy impression that he was being hauled over a series of stone walls. Ocean was to blame for it and the boy kept yelling at him to stop. But he didn't stop.

So they kept going until a sleepy voice said, "Put him in here. I'll report him at sick call."

"Meanwhile he needs a bath," Ocean said. "I will . . ."

"Bath!" the other exploded. "They've just dumped four hundred wounded on us. Do you think we've got time to bathe 'em?"

"No," Ocean answered. "I'll take care of this one."

"Who says so?"

"General Sheridan. And, sonny, if you disobey his orders your hide won't be worth tanning."

Rick came out of a tangle of dreams when reveille sounded. He reached for his shoes and pitched sideways out of bed onto the floor. Bed? He hadn't been in a bed for months. Someone cursed him for making a disturbance and another man laughed at his clumsiness. He stood up and slumped across the cot. A hand reached out and caught his hair. An angry voice threatened, "If you thrash around and hit the stump of my leg, I'll kill you."

"The bugle sounded," Rick mumbled.

"What if it did? Don't you know you're in a hospital?"

"Hospital? What for?"

"Because you're sick, you idiot."

"I don't believe it," Rick whispered, and passed out again.

After that came flashes of action, visions. They made no sense and they were all unpleasant. There were moments when he came out of his make-believe world. At such times he was hot and thirsty. It was usually Ocean who gave him water and bathed his parched skin. Then sickness would sweep over him in a wave and he would go on struggling, among jumbled sights and sounds.

There came a night when he thought he was dead. His mind was suddenly clear, the burning and the thirst were gone and he felt weightless as though floating in space. A few lights shone dimly, like stars. This is it, he concluded without fear. I am on my way to that other world. Somewhere a horse whinnied and Rick tingled all over. They were sending a horse for him! He called as loudly as he could, "Ready! I'm coming!"

"Dry up!" growled a nearby voice.

"Oh!" Rick gasped. "Are — are you alive?"

"It's no thanks to you that I be. You've been yappin' and yellin' in my ear for the past two weeks."

"Two weeks!"

"Shut up! Want to disturb the whole ward, do you? Another word out of you and I'll brain you with this water jug — if you've got a brain."

"I'll spoil your face some day," Rick promised hotly.

"Thank the Lord!" the other said fervently. "The fever's left you and you're talkin' rational." His voice softened. "Better go to sleep now. You'll be weak as a rag for a spell."

When Rick woke up, he saw Ocean looking down at him, thumbs hooked in the armholes of his vest.

"What time is it?" Rick asked.

Ocean pulled out a silver watch and dangled it over a forefinger. "Twelve minutes past four."

"Have I been here all night?"

"Yep."

"Say! I'm in bed? What ails me? I can't sit up."

"That's because you've had acute horizontalitis for the past two weeks."

"Say it in English."

"Flat with fever."

For fifteen days Rick had been in the grip of "army fever," a term that might apply to half a dozen ailments. While delirium possessed him the Army of the Potomac had dug itself in around Petersburg, and Sheridan's cavalry had started refitting at White House Point.

That was the way Ocean told it, but when he left the hospital tent the men on each side of Rick added particulars.

"You must have pull," one said enviously.

"No." Rick closed his eyes, for he felt too weak to talk.

"My eye! The way Pond cossets you!"

"And Sheridan has been here two-three times to see you."

"He always visits his men," Rick said.

"Mebbe so, but he don't give Pond time out to wash us twice a day, set here by the hour 'n' feed us cracked ice 'n' soup 'n' oranges."

"And," the first one continued, "Pond fetched a doctor clear from Norfolk — not an army doctor neither. That cost him plenty."

"Shucks!" Rick muttered and fell asleep.

That was not the last of the remarks. There was seldom when he was awake that Rick was not reminded that he was being favored. It made him furious and he denied it with increasing vigor as he gained strength. He said nothing about it to Ocean, for it was a delicate subject. By tending him almost constantly during his delirium Ocean had undoubtedly saved his life.

He was grateful to the bottom of his heart, though he could not understand why Ocean had done it. Army hospitals had improved tremendously since early in the war, when to enter one was equivalent to a death certificate. Now there were more and better doctors, competent orderlies, a considerable number of nurses, new equipment and abundant medicines. Still, a soldier could not expect the kind of attention Rick had received.

Rick had a country boy's dread of hospitals. It was common knowledge that four times as many men died in them as on the battlefield. When he was able to raise his head he looked at the rows of cots and shuddered at their possibilities. Death was understandable if it came from a bullet when a man was fighting back, but when it moved through a ward, an invisible shopper, choosing this one and that one, it was a horror.

For those who lived, those July days and nights were endless torment. Flies and mosquitoes blackened the tent walls, the beds and the exposed parts of the helpless men. The weather may not have been unusually hot and humid, but the Northerners thought it was and cursed it, along with everything else in the South. Wherever their homes were, that was where the air was always sweet, the streams always sparkling, people always kind. They were sick and tired of war, fed up with the bickering and blundering of generals. They wanted to go home. And from what they had learned from prisoners, they knew the Johnnies felt the same way about it. Everyone wanted to go home.

At the end of three weeks Rick asked for his uniform and struggled into it. Though it fitted like a sack, he was proud of it because someone had sewn his "pumpkin rind" stripes on the sleeve. That gave him strength to walk out of the tent.

"Where are thee going?" an orderly demanded.

"To my quarters."

"Have thee been discharged?"

"Sure."

"Where are thy papers?"

"To thunder with my papers."

"Thee can't work thy special privilege game here."

"I'm sick of that." Rick began to sweat. "What's more, I am an officer and I don't take orders from you."

"Forgive me — sir." The orderly grinned.

Rick suddenly noticed how pale and tired the fellow looked. "I didn't mean to be crusty," the new lieutenant said. "It's just that I can't stand any more hospital."

"I don't blame thee. I am starting my fourth year of it."

"You're a Quaker. Why did you go in?"

"The spirit moved me." The orderly re-entered the tent.

Rick dragged himself along, with frequent rests, until he found Ocean sitting under a tree mending a stirrup strap.

"Nice day for a walk, boy."

Rick said nothing until he was down on the grass, then he asked, "Did the spirit move you to enlist?"

"No, it was the sheriff."

"Liar. What about when you re-enlisted?"

"Same sheriff. Why?"

"I wonder why we do those things. I haven't found a man who doesn't hate war, yet here we are, and we're staying."

"Yes." Ocean rubbed an oiled rag on the strap. "Something makes us. Some call it patriotism, some call it love of adventure, some don't call it anything because they aren't handy with words."

"I did a lot of thinking while I was sick."

"You are still sick. You should have a month's leave."

"That's too much to hope for," Rick said wistfully.

But he kept hoping. It would be heaven to get away from the sights and sounds and smells of camp for a while. Once he had loved such things, now he hated them. He might as well admit he was no use in his present condition, so he would not be shirking if he had some leave. Leave, however, was hard to get unless a man were seriously wounded or had been in service a long time. A convalescent, who had been in only a few months, was usually told to take it easy for a time and then get back in line.

Rick understood this and throughout July made a grim effort to pull himself together. But he could not shake off his lassitude. Day after day he reported sick at roll call and the company doctor knew he was not pretending. His strength was coming back, but his ambition, as he told Ocean, was as dormant as a woodchuck in winter.

Ocean tried, and failed, to interest him in the war. And there was plenty of it to think about. Thanks to General Burnside's bungling, the Union forces had failed to take Richmond and were bogged down in the trenches outside Petersburg. Tough old General Jubal Early had scattered what Yankees remained in the Shenandoah Valley and forged within sight of Washington before Grant could send enough men to stop him. Now there were four small Union armies marching and countermarching between the two capitals, the commanders of each issuing contradictory orders to the others, while the War Department in Washington overruled them all. Grant wanted to unify those four commands but was blocked by politicians. Then the Confederates showed up in Pennsylvania and began burning and looting.

Everyone in the Army of the Potomac knew these things soon after they happened, and there was an angry buzzing, especially in the camp at Sheridan's headquarters. But Rick had no part in it. He lay in his tent steeped in the lethargy he no longer wanted to combat. During the afternoon of August third he dragged himself over to the hospital for his quota of medicine. Just inside the tent he met the Quaker orderly, who waved an envelope at him.

"The order for thy leave!" he sang out. "A month in Washington, all arrangements made by the Sanitary Commission. Thee are fortunate, friend."

"I'm a lucky dog." Rick straightened up and smiled for the first time in weeks. "You fellows keep the war going while I'm away."

"Sure," a voice sneered behind him. "Anything to make it easier for you."

And another added, "It must be nice to have friends at H.Q."

"I don't ask any odds from you," Rick roared at them. He went out, his ears burning.

He was on his way to tell Ocean the good news when Captain Mike Sheridan burst out of the telegrapher's tent in long strides.

"Big news, O'Shay!" he shouted. "Lincoln has agreed to Grant's plan to consolidate all the troops from here to Washington — about forty-five thousand. It's called the Army of the Shenandoah, and my little brother Phil is its commander!"

"Whew!" Rick stopped in his tracks. Again, after a long bitter month, he felt the joy of life leaping in his veins.

"We'll see some action worth writing home about." Mike waved his cap. "We start for the Shenandoah at once."

"Yes, sir!"

Rick saluted briskly. Then he tore his sick leave papers in small pieces and watched them scatter to the wind.

IF GENERAL SHERIDAN KNEW RICK REFUSED SICK LEAVE, and he had amazing ability to remember details concerning his men, he did not mention it. On the other hand the Yankee troopers were surprisingly well informed about him and his problems because they were avid newspaper readers and had had the benefits of the free schools in the North. Every campfire was a lyceum where questions of state and military strategy were freely discussed and where many a leader's reputation was made or broken.

When Grant created the new Army of the Shenandoah, the men understood fairly well what Sheridan was up against. First, many of the big shots, including President Lincoln and Secretary of War Stanton, thought he was too young for the job. The presidential election was coming up in November and as sure as the new general was defeated in the Shenandoah Valley — as every Union commander there had been — the North would be so discouraged that Lincoln's renomination would be doubtful. If he were defeated, the odds were ten to one the war would end in a draw, and the agony of the past four years would have been in vain.

General Grant understood all this and, though it made him wince to consider it, he knew what he must do. The Valley, as it was called, was one of the most beautiful spots on earth. Some sixty miles wide in places, it lay between the Alleghenies and the Blue Ridge Mountains, a garden spot if there ever was one. Because it was peopled mostly by Quakers, Mennonites and other religious sects who were splendid farmers but refused to fight, it had plenty of man-power to till its fields and make it, all through the war, the granary of the Confederacy. Men like Robert E. Lee and Stonewall Jackson and Jubal Early had been able to keep the Yankees out of the Valley for the most part. Lee was keenly aware that if it were lost his army and the city of Richmond would be starved and the war might be over.

Fate had placed Grant, one of the most humane of men, in an agonizing position. He was convinced that everything in the Valley contributing aid to the enemy must be de-stroyed. It would be terrible, yet less terrible than prolong-ing the war. He was sure that Phil Sheridan, another hu-manitarian at heart, was the one to strike the blow.

Grant wrote the orders in words that could not be mis-understood. To Halleck, chief of staff in Washington, he sent the now historic message to clean out the Valley "so that crows flying over it for the balance of the season will have to carry their provender with them." To Sheridan, who would have the order read before the troops, he was equally emphatic and directed that after defeating the forces, "Take all provisions, forage, and stock wanted for the use

of your command. Such as cannot be consumed, destroy
. . . Make all the valley a desert . . . Loyal citizens can
bring in their claims against the government for this necessary destruction. No houses will be burned, and officers in
charge of this delicate but necessary duty must inform the
people that the object is to make this valley untenable for
the raiding parties of the Rebel army."

As usual, Sheridan did not waste a minute. Even before
he and Grant had completed all their plans, he had ordered
his scattered forces to converge at Halltown, near the lower
end of the Valley. Sheridan rode over from Harper's Ferry,
and, as he held Rienzi to that famous five-miles-an-hour
walk along the crowded roads, his quick eyes saw Rick directing traffic at a junction.

"Lieutenant O'Shay!" He pulled over, for he was not
one to halt a line. "Have the doctors given you your liberty?"

"Yes, sir." Rick blushed with pleasure as he saluted.

"Good! I have work for you at headquarters."

That was his way; he was your commander and your
friend. He made you feel that he and you were partners.
Rick thought, how good it is to be back with him! What
ever made me think of going on sick leave? This is the medicine for me.

Sheridan knew it would take at least a month to coordi-
nate the elements of his new army and get it working
smoothly. He needed the time because sooner or later Lee
would send reinforcements to Early and then fighting would

be resumed in the Valley. Meanwhile, Sheridan would advance slowly, working out details as he went.

Those reinforcements showed up in mid-August, whereat Grant, as part of his overall strategy, ordered Sheridan to fall back to a strong position near Halltown and await developments. The Northern newspapers, unable to understand what Grant was up to, went all out in calling Little Phil fainthearted, if not downright cowardly.

"What do you think about all this howling in the papers, Ocean?" Rick asked.

"The people who write for the papers know that every Union commander who went into the Valley was licked there — Banks, Shields, Fremont, Sigel and Hunter. Now that Sheridan has backed up they naturally think he's afraid of the same treatment."

"But he will not be licked," Rick said stoutly.

"Probably not. Justin Morgan wasn't created so that one of his line could help Phil Sheridan run away."

"You are plumb silly about that horse."

"All right, all right, all right! You don't have to take my word for it that Rienzi will have a big part in winning this war. Wait and see it happen." Ocean stalked away.

While the army moved up the Valley and then back, it carried on the cruel work of destruction. Nothing like it had been seen before. From one line of mountains to the other, clear across that beautiful land so rich with crops and cattle, the Blue cavalry ranged, while infantry and artillery guarded the roads against surprise attack. Every barn, and there were hundreds of them in the big Pennsylvania Dutch style, every mill and every bridge was burned. Every head of livestock and every kernel of grain, except such as was needed to keep the farmers from starving, was eaten by the army or destroyed.

Before laying waste a farm, an officer determined how much food its owner might keep. Such exemptions varied according to the judgment, or charity, of that particular Yankee. Most of the officers hated the job. They did it because it was orders and because they understood it was the quickest way to starve the Confederate army. It was war, and yet when they saw God-fearing farmers, women, children and old people, begging to keep what they had rightfully earned by years of labor, they questioned among themselves if it was war. And as they tramped along or bivouacked there was none of the usual gaiety of soldiers. In the Valley, now darkened by the smoke of homesteads, they wondered how they would feel if this thing were happening in Vermont, or Michigan, or Iowa.

To many of them, including Rick, the real tragedy was that such work seemed necessary. Once, neither side would have employed such tactics; there was decency and gallantry in them then. Now, much of it was gone and in its place was a meanness that rationalized the suffering of noncombatants. Barns and haystacks and cattle could be replaced, but the legacy of hate would endure for a long while.

Rick soon learned that the most vicious role in the Valley was being played by the guerrillas. They were bands of outlaws, often made up of deserters and draft-dodgers from both sides, who posed as friends of the South. Some hid out in the mountains, others pretended to be peaceful farmers, and all lived by plundering. Their spies were everywhere and many a soldier in gray or blue passed the word when good spoil was around. Then the raiders gathered in the dark and swooped upon some weakly guarded Union wagon train, horse corral or supply depot. They were merciless killers, capable of stampeding seasoned troops. Usually they were able to make off with the loot and disappear. When dressed in Federal uniforms they plundered the Valley inhabitants and, sometimes, even the Confederates they were supposed to support. Few Southerners acknowledged them and such generals as Lee and Stuart were vigorous in their denouncements.

When Sheridan came to the Valley these renegades raised his ire. Custer was the man to handle them and Sheridan sent him out after them. The long-haired daredevil made one of his spectacular swoops and caught two guerrillas who had robbed a Quaker family. They were promptly hanged. A few days later he galloped up to a crossroads tavern, shot two others and picked up four more before they could change from the Federal uniforms they were wearing. These too were strung up and left as a warning.

Sheridan was grimly pleased. However, he was troubled by the possibility that the hot-headed Custer might make a mistake, and hang a Confederate soldier or a peaceable Valley resident. He ordered Custer to call off the hunt for a while. A week later a small detachment of Union infantry guarding a telegraph station received orders by wire, obviously from field headquarters, directing them to take a short cut through the woods and join a supply train that was coming up. Next day a Mennonite boy in the neighborhood told how he had seen the little company ambushed by a hundred horsemen. When the fight was over every Yankee was dead, including eight prisoners they had taken who had been hanged to one tree.

The Union camp boiled with fury. In any army it was murder to execute a soldier who had not been condemned by court martial. No Confederate officer would have done such a thing. It had a guerrilla stench. What was more, it must have been planned by a spy or a traitor in the Federal ranks.

Sheridan had dismounted and was talking with Ocean when Captain Mike told him the news. The general roared so that Rienzi jumped. His face grew so dark that Ocean's ruddy cheeks looked pale by comparison.

"The unspeakable — the — the . . ." He clenched both fists over his head. "They murdered my boys! Murdered them! You must be mistaken, Mike. You must be!"

"No, Phil. The bodies have been recovered. There was a note pinned on one: 'We pay our debts.' "

"Debts!" The general's face was so terrible that Rick breathed fast. "When I learn who betrayed my boys I'll pay my debts. I'll hang him, even if he is my own brother."

No one else spoke until after the two Sheridans had walked away together.

"This is getting to be a meaner war every day." Ocean wagged his head. "It's making criminals of all of us."

"Guerrillas would have been criminals anyway," Rick said.

"Some would, some wouldn't. Men are doing things to-day they would have been ashamed to do a few years ago. One man wears a blue coat and is a hero. Another wears a gray coat and is a wicked rebel. A third wears no coat and is a guerrilla. But all are in the same business — killing their brothers. Flags and uniforms! According to the color, you are noble or fit to be hanged."

"You're not defending guerrillas, are you?" Rick cried.

"No! If a man must kill, the sin is less if he remains loyal to one side — or the other."

Again Rick had the uneasy feeling that Ocean was being ambiguous about his allegiance. It was silly but the thought persisted.

A few days later it returned in a way that could not be ignored. Rick was off duty one afternoon and in the mood for a nap. His blanket was wet because he had upset a pail of water after breakfast. He lay down in Ocean's tent, knowing its owner had ridden over to look at a horse of General Custer's that was sick. Rick stretched out on the blanket and felt a hard lump under his head. He moved to one side and went to sleep, only to wake up with the lump digging into his ear. It felt like a pebble and, being only half awake, he imagined Ocean had put it there to annoy him. He sat up angrily and pulled back the blanket.

The lump was a brass button on the carefully folded uniform of a Confederate colonel.

☆ 12 ☆

RICK STARED AT THE UNIFORM AS THOUGH HE HAD NEVER seen one. Confederate gray was common enough, both on the living and the dead, and many Yankee soldiers boasted some among their souvenirs. But they paraded it and invented wild stories about it; they did not hide a Confederate coat under their blankets.

Rick covered the uniform and went back to his own tent, feeling guilty. He told himself it was none of his business how Ocean came by the thing or what he did with it. A man had a right to his own property and people who went snooping around in tents when the owners were absent were only one degree better than thieves. He had known it to happen many times in the army and when the guilty ones were caught . . . His act had not been premeditated, but he shouldn't have been there in the first place.

He felt so mean about it that at first he decided to confess as soon as Ocean returned. The little devils of suspicion went to work. His memory went back to the night in New York when he first sensed something devious in Ocean's behavior. Since then there had been other incidents, small ones and perhaps of no importance, but all adding up to the possibility that Ocean might be pro-Southern. And now, at the very moment when the camp was seething with spy talk, came his discovery of the hidden uniform.

It was the first time Rick had been squarely up against the problem of doubting a friend's loyalty. Few things are more unpleasant. General Sheridan had trusted Ocean for years. That should have been enough, but it did not dispel Rick's suspicions. However, he had no doubts on one score, it would take a lot more to make him openly question one who had befriended him since he first entered the army and who had recently nursed him back to life. Gratitude laid him under a deep obligation.

The next day Ocean was about again. Come to think of it, he had been away several times since the Shenandoah campaign opened. Rick tried to satisfy himself with the thought that Sheridan must know about it or there would have been fireworks when Ocean was not there to care for Rienzi. Anyhow, it was not for a lieutenant to question the commanding general.

In the afternoon Sheridan paraded some of the troops. They were Hunter's men, those who had returned after running away to West Virginia. He put them through their paces in a way that made his veterans smile. Then he went to his tent to write letters, telling Rick to stay around in case he was needed.

As Rick stood there in the lazy sunshine of early autumn, it seemed impossible he was surrounded by war. The illusion of peace was so strong that the old Quaker farmer trudging toward Sheridan's tent seemed a natural part of it until Rick remembered with a start where he was.

"Halt!" he ordered, as he stepped in front of the man. "Where are you going?"

"To appeal to General Sheridan, friend," the old man answered. His face was haggard and his eyes held a look of weary suffering.

"You can't walk into the general's tent that way," Rick told him. "Don't you know a war is going on?"

"Yes." The Quaker did not flinch. "Will thee ask General Sheridan if he will speak to a United States citizen in the name of mercy?"

"I am afraid the general is busy now."

"I will wait. Will thee permit me to sit down?"

"You do look tuckered out." Rick noticed that the old man's knees were trembling. "Go over there in the shade and take it easy."

"Thee will not forget to speak to General Sheridan?"

"No, when he has time."

"What is it, O'Shay?" Sheridan stepped out of his tent. As always, when on foot, his short legs and long arms were noticeably disproportionate. "Oh, I see. What is it, my friend?"

The Quaker looked him in the eye. "General Sheridan, my wife is sore sick. Thy soldiers have burned our barn, taken our cattle, destroyed our crops and left us nothing to eat."

"No!" Sheridan scowled. "Give me the name of the

officer who did that. He signed a requisition paper, didn't he?"

"No." The Quaker reached out and steadied himself against a tree.

"Are you sure he wasn't a guerrilla in disguise?"

"He spoke like a Northerner."

Sheridan's lips tightened. He eyed the old man closely and then asked, "When did you eat last?"

"It was — some days ago, General."

"Come in here. I will get you something." Sheridan turned toward the tent.

The Quaker put up a hand in protest. "If thee means food, may I carry it to my wife?"

"There is enough for you both. O'Shay, order a mule team ready to start immediately. Come inside, my friend, and tell me what food and medicines you need to see you through the winter."

"General, I am not begging for myself."

"Begging! We take what you have saved during a lifetime — and still you are not bitter. You don't curse us and this war we are waging. Still you have Christian fortitude. I wish there were fifty million 'beggars' like you in this country." Sheridan's teeth snapped together.

During the next half hour the business of running the Army of the Shenandoah was secondary to Sheridan's efforts to cheer an unknown old man and his ailing wife. He fed the Quaker at his camp table, slicing his bread and meat for him and cutting off a wedge of pound cake Mrs. Custer had sent in from Harper's Ferry. He talked a stream, asking many questions and pacing the tent. The plight of the Valley had always touched him deeply and now it was epitomized by this heroic farmer.

"How I hate the word 'war,' " he said passionately. "Destruction — suffering — inexcusable in the sight of the Almighty."

"Thee forgets," the old man answered, "that the Crucifixion was ordained to precede the Resurrection."

Sheridan stared at him. "You can say that after what you have been through?"

"Yes, friend."

Sheridan took the knotted hand in both of his. "Friend," he spoke the word reverently, "I have wondered many times where I could find strength to carry out this task. You have given me the answer. Thank you." He lighted his pipe and puffed furiously.

The Quaker stood up and looked down at the little general. "Thee are a good man, Friend Sheridan," he said.

The general saw to loading the wagon, then ordered Lieutenant O'Shay to take six troopers and convoy it to the Quaker's farm three miles away. Rick tried to look modest but he was throbbing with pride, for it was his first command. Up to then he had been a mere messenger, but now he was being trusted to handle men. He rode ahead of the wagon beside the Quaker, looking very businesslike and wishing there were more people around to see him. Of the thousands of lieutenants, none felt more important and more sure of himself than Rick.

He completed his mission at the farm and started back in the twilight. The crossroad they were using led through a little valley less than a rifle-shot wide, open at both ends and fringed by heavy undergrowth. It would be a nice place for an ambush, but it was too near the line for that to happen. Still, it would impress the men, Rick decided, if he showed them he understood his business. He ordered two to stay with the wagon, two to scout to the right and one to follow him to the left. It was fine for a large train, but a perfect way to split his tiny force into helpless fragments.

Rick's horse dropped before the first shot sounded. He jumped clear and yelled to charge, as though they were a whole company. But the trooper was already on the grass in a lifeless heap. Rick slid sideways on his face and emptied his carbine at the bushes on the hill where puffs of smoke were showing. He twisted around and saw other puffs on the opposite side of the road. A riderless horse was over there and the mule team was running away. Thump! a rifle ball hit the ground close to his head, throwing dirt in his eyes. He brushed it away with one hand and reached for his revolver.

When he came to, he thought he was being rolled over a barrel that was bumping down the hill. Then he realized he was face down on a galloping horse, his wrists and ankles tied to the stirrups. He could not raise his head and all he could see was the ground that seemed to be flowing under him. He felt no pain and could not guess where he was or how he got there.

"Hey!" he yelled as loudly as he could. "What do you think you are doing?"

For a moment thudding hoofs were the only answer, then a voice said, "Shut yer mouth!" and something hard and flat like the flat of a saber slapped down on the seat of his trousers.

Rick had never been so mad, not even at Ed Potts. He struggled until he was out of breath, which did not take long because the horse was trotting now, pounding the boy's belly unmercifully and making his head roar. Darkness set in, but he could not tell if it were natural or caused by blood pressure in his eyes. If this kept up much longer something would have to give.

Somewhere an order was given and the horses stood still.

"What now, Shep?" a voice asked.

"Git out the lanterns. Then untie him. Is he still kickin'?"

Rick didn't like Shep's voice. Neither did he like the way unseen hands untied him and let him slip to the ground like a sack, for his feet were numb.

"Git up," Shep ordered.

Rick sat up. "How did you knock me out without hitting me?"

"Barked ye, same as I'd bark a squirrel on a limb — shoot so close to his head he's stunned. It was a accident with you. Now git up."

Rick stood and looked around. The darkness was disturbed by swaying lanterns as several men came out of what appeared to be a barn. They gathered around the prisoner in the half-light, the shadows from their slouch hats falling across their bearded faces. Shep, the leader, was young and slim, with something of a soldierly bearing, though he wore no uniform. Without question they were guerrillas.

The last man held his lantern high. "You!"

Rick stiffened as he recognized Ed Potts.

"Hain't you glad to see me?" Ed grinned in his foolish way.

"As glad as I ever was," Rick answered.

"Shep," Ed became very important, "I want this feller. He's the one I told ye tied me to a tree at Cold Harbor fight."

"That's a lie," Rick said hotly. "The boys tied you up after they caught you robbing the dead. I didn't do it."

"I want that feller, Shep." Ed took a step forward.

"Keep back," Shep growled.

"You don't know who he is." Ed held his ground. "He's Gen'ral Sheridan's pet. The gen'ral would jest blow up if anything happened to his little cosset lamb."

Rick lunged at him, but Shep and two others held him back. Then they tied his hands.

"You know he is a stinker." Rick addressed Shep. "He's a coward, a grave robber and a deserter."

"Yeh," Shep said casually, as though such things were common. "What's this about you 'n' Sheridan being friends?"

"I am one of his aides, that's all."

"He has a liking for you?"

"Why, perhaps so. But generals don't get thick with lieutenants."

"Yank," Shep snapped. "I don't hold no grudge against you, but I hold a big one against Phil Sheridan. He just hung some of my friends, so I've got to do the same by him."

"You mean you are — are going to — to hang me?"

"Yeh. I'll give you ten minutes to git ready." Shep disappeared in the dark.

Rick's first thought was to try to escape, even if his hands were bound. His knees were weak, but he could get hold of himself in a minute. He glanced cautiously around the circle of silent guerrillas, calculating which two lanterns he would kick out as he made his dash. The men might cut him down with their sabers, but that would be better than hanging. Rick had hardened himself to accept all kinds of death in battle, but this was a horror he had never before imagined.

He closed his eyes for a moment, and then he cried aloud as a noose was slipped over his head from behind and drawn quickly around his neck.

"You promised me ten minutes," he choked.

"You'll have it," Shep said. "I'm just areadying things." He tossed the other end of the rope over a branch and stood holding it.

Ed Potts stepped close to Rick and held a lantern high. Rick bowed his head because he could not endure that grin of triumph. He hated himself for being afraid, but he could

not find the courage to overcome it. He tried to think of
something heroic to say, as Nathan Hale had done, and he
realized there was nothing heroic in him. He was pitifully
scared and alone. Judge Meader, Ocean Pond, even Sheridan himself could not help him.

"Ye don't look so pert as ye used to," Ed mocked him.
"I'm awful sorry for ye, Rick. Tell ye what I'll do, if you'll
git down on yer knees 'n' beg me real hard I'll talk to Shep.
Will ye beg?"

"No!" Rick's head snapped up and his eyes blazed. "I'll
never get on my knees to you or any other coward."

He was no longer alone and afraid. Someone was with
him. Someone sweeter than life and stronger than death,
who told him not to fear. He did not struggle when they
put him on a horse and tightened the rope on the branch
above his head. The horse would be led from under him in
another moment, but he sat straight and quiet.

☆ 13 ☆

"HEADS UP, FRIENDS OF THE CONFEDERACY!" THE WORDS rang through the dark woods. Instantly there was a shifting of lights and the sound of firearms being cocked.

"Who goes there?" Shep challenged.

"A friend."

"Come in. Keep him covered, boys."

A man stepped into the light, his arms half raised to show he was empty handed. He was slightly built and wore the uniform of a Confederate colonel. He removed his black slouch hat and smiled with one corner of his mouth.

"Colonel Pond, C. S. A.," he announced. "At your service, gentlemen." He saluted.

Rick hugged the horse with his knees to keep from swaying.

Shep returned the salute. "Captain Shepard, sir. We're about to carry out the order of the court." He indicated the prisoner.

"Court-martial proceedings, I suppose," Ocean said indifferently.

"Same sort of court-martial Phil Sheridan gave our boys." Shep raised his lantern to show the rope.

Rick did not dare breathe as he and Ocean eyed each other.

"You have a prize here," Ocean said to Shep. "This Yank is Lieutenant O'Shay, one of Sheridan's pets."

"That's just what I told 'em," Ed put in. "I've knowed him all my life."

"Indeed." The Confederate officer did not seem interested in the guerrilla. But he explained to Captain Shepard, "My work is mostly behind the lines, as General Early can testify. This man O'Shay is better informed than some of Sheridan's staff."

"That's what we're wanting," Shep said. "Little old Phil is going to squawk when he hears we put a hemp ribbon round his baby boy's neck."

The men laughed and Ocean twisted his mouth in an appreciative smile as he agreed, "He'll be the maddest banty rooster on earth."

"Then the sooner the better." Shep raised his hand to lead the horse from under Rick.

"Your pardon, Captain." Ocean stopped him with a gesture. "This Yank possesses information of great value to General Early. May I question him?"

"Is that a order, Colonel?"

"I prefer to call it a favor, Captain, a favor to the Confederacy."

"How long'll it take?"

"Perhaps all night, if the Yank is stubborn."

"You promise we can swing him by daylight, sir?"

"I give you my word the examination will be finished by then."

There were grumblers, but Shep talked to them in a low voice. After all, it would be to their advantage to accommodate the colonel, for they were not too favorably regarded in some Confederate quarters. It wouldn't do a bit of harm if word reached General Early that they were helping the cause. So Shep had them take the rope from Rick's neck and let him stand on his own feet.

"It'll give you more time to say your prayers," Ed jeered at him.

"See to the horses, Potts," Shep ordered. And when Ed had gone, still snickering at his own wit, he said, "Our men aren't all that sort, sir. A Yank is always bad enough, but a renegade Yank stinks."

"The fleas go with the dog," Ocean said. "Speaking of horses, mine is tied a short distance away. I'll fetch him — along with ten pounds of coffee, if that interests you and your men."

"Coffee! Lord, sir, we haven't tasted coffee for months."

"You will tonight — all you want of it."

"Colonel, you-all can have anything we have."

"All I want is a chance to talk with your prisoner. Then you are welcome to hang him." Ocean walked briskly into the woods.

"Come along, Yank," Shep ordered, cocking his revolver. "Head for the barn. There is still one barn Sheridan hasn't burned."

"I never burned a barn," Rick said, as they went along.

Several lanterns hung from beams. By their light Shep tied Rick securely to a post and put a guard over him.

"Anything I can do to make you comfortable?" the captain asked, in almost a pleasant voice.

"Yes, keep that yellow-bellied Potts out of my sight. I'd rather have a rattlesnake in the room."

Shep smiled for the first time. "He fought on your side, Yank."

"He never fought on either side. He's too yellow to fight. I'm glad he deserted to you Rebs, if that's what you call yourselves. He'll add to your troubles."

Shep walked out of the barn and shouted, "Potts!"

"Over here," Ed answered.

"I've told you to address me as sir."

"Yes, sir." Ed's voice cringed.

"Post yourself at the crossroads. If you hear anything suspicious, fire two shots."

"What about the coffee I was to have?"

"You'll get your share later. Now move!"

"Yes, sir."

Rick searched for a weak spot in his bonds — there was none; he was tied tightly and the guard watched him every moment — he speculated desperately on what Ocean was trying to do. Was he loyal or was he a Confederate spy? Was it possible he had fooled General Sheridan? It was hard to believe that. Then — equally hard to believe — had he fooled General Early, one of the most astute officers in the

Rebel army? No matter what he was, could he still be counted a friend? Once the boy would have staked his life on that friendship, but things had happened and were happening to change old values. When a fellow was literally at the end of a rope every possibility was vitally significant.

The sweat of torment was on Rick's face as he waited. He was helpless. Storybook heroes got themselves out of the shadow of death, but there was a difference between a story and being in a hangman's noose!

He heard a sudden clamor from the men outside and the word "coffee" repeated excitedly. Rick knew from what prisoners had said that the Confederacy was starved for coffee. It was almost priceless and what little of it got through the blockade was kept for invalids. When officers weren't around, Southern pickets swapped anything they owned for a handful of the beans.

Rick heard the rattle of kettles and tin cups, the pouring of water and the crackling of a fire. Finally the aroma of boiling coffee drifted into the barn. "Fill them up!" He heard Ocean invite them. Not a word had been said about price.

"Aooow!" A cry of pain split the darkness. "It's boiling!" Ocean choked.

"Burn you, suh?" Shep inquired politely.

"My gullet is scalded."

"You dropped your cup, sir."

"Never mind. I can't drink anything hot for a month." Ocean stamped into the barn, his mouth wide open. "Go get your coffee, boy," he said to the guard. "I will take your place here."

"Obliged, sir." The man was off.

Rick trembled. Now was the time, if ever, for Ocean to cut him loose. But Ocean did not even look his way, just stood there blowing from his open mouth.

"Ocean!" Rick whispered.

Ocean gave him a cold look. "When Captain Shepard returns we will question you," he said stiffly. "Until then be silent."

"You double-dyed old renegade!" Rick said distinctly. "I hope Phil Sheridan hangs you to the tallest tree in Virginia and leaves you there for the crows."

Ocean's face blazed. He reached for his revolver, then pulled back and without a word gagged Rick with a handkerchief. After that he ignored the prisoner. But Rick did not ignore him. He kept his eyes on the face that once had seemed so kindly, but was now the face of one who had betrayed his country and double-crossed his friends.

Strangely enough, when time was going so fast Rick forgot its passage. He only knew that after a while the sounds outside the barn diminished and then stopped. Ocean disappeared, then came back whistling a tune.

"You know, Rick," he said, in his old whimsical style, "there was a man who lost a parrot down a dry well, cage and all. She was there three days before they found her. 'Were you lonesome down there, Polly?' they asked her, after she was fished up. 'No,' she croaked, 'but it was a blamed long night.' That's what you must think, boy." He took out the gag and slashed the ropes with his saber.

"Let's get out of here," said Rick.

"There is no special hurry, the boys are asleep. It just happens that that Reb colonel who was around here dropped some laudanum in their coffee. They'll sleep for hours. Come, take a look." He led the way out of the barn.

The guerrillas lay about on the grass. Even Shep, who should have known better, had succumbed to the irresistible lure of coffee.

"Are you going to finish them off?" Rick asked, thinking of what they would have done to him.

"I can't kill in cold blood," Ocean said. "Can you?"

"I suppose not. But they don't deserve to go free."

"We'll see that they don't. Pick up their guns, then give me a hand." Ocean began cutting a picket rope into short lengths.

"I'll fetch a team and we will haul them back to camp before they come to." Ocean chuckled. "It's the unexpected things that add spice to life. Meanwhile, Rick, you hang around and make sure your friend Potts doesn't come back for his coffee."

"I wish he was here," Rick said. "Why did he have to be the one to escape!"

"Shep thought he was doing you a favor. Well, I'll be off. My horse isn't far away." Ocean faded into the darkness.

Rick still wondered about Ocean and fervently wished that this night would end.

It finally did and with the dawn came a troop of Union cavalry escorting a mule wagon. They were guided by

Ocean, who once more wore his old blue uniform. The outlaws were still too dopey to realize they were being loaded
in and carted away. Their belongings, from horses to tin
cups, were collected, and the barn was burned.

"That cleans out that hornets' nest," a trooper said with
satisfaction. "Nice work, Lieutenant."

"The credit all goes to Pond," Rick said, glancing at
Ocean.

"How did he manage it?"

"I don't know," Rick answered truthfully.

"Didn't he tell you?"

"Not half of it." Rick rode away.

☆ 14 ☆

Rick was in a quandary about Ocean. Obviously Ocean was playing a game, but Rick felt assured he was playing it in accordance with his own code of honor.

After what had taken place, Rick found himself bound by a code of his own to keep quiet. He resolved to act as though Ocean was one hundred per cent Union, until he had sound reason for thinking otherwise.

Meanwhile, Northern newspapers were berating Sheridan for not finishing, or trying to finish, the job he had started in the Valley. Thoughtful people the world over were saying that unless one of the Union armies rang up a victory very soon, Abraham Lincoln could not carry the November election and the war would be lost. Yankee politicians ranted, with some apparent reason, that Grant was a senseless butcher, Sheridan an irresponsible young roughneck and that Lincoln had ruined everything by giving them such vital commands. The President and the two generals said nothing, which convinced their critics they had nothing to say.

But there came a day in mid-September when Grant

asked Sheridan to meet him in Charlestown. A council of war is usually thought of as taking place in a building, or at least a tent, and as being attended by a group of officers, with gold braid and flags. This one was different. Two men in an open field paced back and forth together. Their uniforms as usual were dusty. A few aides sat their horses at a respectful distance, one holding Rienzi, the other a little black pacer named Jeff Davis. Some infantrymen leaned on a rail fence chewing tobacco.

Sheridan did most of the talking and all of the gesturing. Grant walked beside him, looking at the ground, his shoulders hunched. Ashes from his cigar littered his unbuttoned coat and vest. Finally Sheridan stopped talking and began filling his little pipe. Grant looked suddenly at the sky as though seeing something written there, then Rick and the others heard him say sharply, "Go in."

Those two words made history, and to a considerable extent they made Philip Sheridan. He and Grant had each worked out a plan for the forthcoming Valley campaign, and with characteristic courtesy the older man allowed him to speak first. Grant listened and then never took his own plan out of his pocket. From then on the Army of the Shenandoah was entirely in the hands of Little Phil.

He knew what to do with it.

"This army is being coiled like a bull whip," Rick said, at the end of a day of ceaseless activity. "Heaven pity the Valley when Sheridan lashes out."

"It won't be long now." Ocean said. "Let's have one

more leisurely meal before the storm breaks. Come over to supper and we'll have roast goose."

"Wow!" Rick grinned in anticipation. "Where did you find a goose?"

"I haven't," Ocean said. "But I found a gooseberry. If I throw the berry away there is bound to be a goose left, isn't there?"

"Oh, I see. You are worried about this campaign."

"It's so vital it scares me, Rick. It may swing the war."

"Well, we'll wait and see."

"We may see, but we won't wait," Ocean said grimly. "The days of waiting are over."

True. An hour after midnight the army began moving toward Winchester, around which Early's command was concentrated. "Old Jubilee," as he was called, was betting his splendid reputation he could whip the Yankees on his own ground. He had done it before. The fact that Phil Sheridan was there this time was of no consequence. He was just one more to be swept into the ash heap. If a poll could have been taken, a heavy majority of Southerners and Northerners would have agreed with him.

A striking exception to this feeling of pessimism was the army itself. No one quite knew what had happened, but there was a new spirit abroad in the ranks. That day soldiers did not slog along because they had to, they marched with a will and when Sheridan galloped past they cheered. He waved his hat and yelled back a snappy man-to-man greeting. Perhaps that was it. For years the Yankees had seen

their top brass seldom and then only at a distance. Here was
a two-star general who was with them all the while, watching them, scolding them, praising them and leading them in
battle. Now he wanted to clean the Johnnies out of the Valley and they were with him to a man.

Rick had been on duty all night and at dawn was watering
his horse in Opequon Creek, where the last of the army was
crossing. In the west, some six miles away, he heard the
pulse-quickening rumble of guns as Early opened up on the
Union vanguard. Ocean rode up carrying Sheridan's little
personal flag, a red-and-white swallowtail with the major-
general's two stars.

"I've traipsed all over the sapworks looking for you," he
said. "You're to carry this today. Take this horse, he's fresh.
You'll need three others to keep up with Rienzi. You'll find
the general on the Berryville road in a temper. Get along!"

"How does it happen I carry the flag?" Rick asked, as he
stepped from one saddle to the other.

"You're his handy man. If you get shot dead don't you
dare drop that flag. He won't accept excuses today."

Sheridan had reason for blowing off. He had ordered a
considerable part of the cavalry and three infantry divisions
to march from Berryville to Winchester. It was a narrow
highway and for three miles it ran through a steep-sided ravine, a natural bottleneck. To forestall a jam he had explicitly
told the troops to leave their baggage behind and move fast.
The plan was working smoothly when one of those things
happened that no one can ever explain. The entire baggage

train of one corps crawled into the defile, slowing the next corps to a snail's pace and causing a terrific tie-up. Even the infantry could not climb around it because the banks were so steep. The battle had already begun in Winchester and might be lost right there unless reinforcements could be brought up.

Sheridan and Rienzi hit the jam like a tornado. Dripping sweat and shooting fire from wild eyes, man and horse crashed into the tangle. "Ditch the damn wagons!" the general roared. "Let those troops through now! Hurry up! Hurry up! Hurry up!" Rienzi lunged, teeth bared, at the first wagon team and in a matter of minutes the whole train was in the ditch, part of it upside down. The infantry was passing it at a run. As Rick tore after Sheridan, carrying the little flag proudly, he heard rousing cheers, and he thought even the teamsters joined in.

By reason of his new job, Rick saw more of the battle than did most of the soldiers. Much of it he could not comprehend and he had no time to study it. His business was to keep that flag close behind Rienzi so everyone might know the exact whereabouts of the general. That was such a busy assignment he had little leisure to speculate why Sheridan did this or that, or why he did not stop a bullet, when men were falling by hundreds all around him.

He did understand that the delay in the ravine nearly cost them the battle, by giving the Confederates time to get set. It was noon and the Rebels charged so viciously that a whole Yankee division was put in wild retreat. When Rick saw men throw down their guns and run, while the madly yelling enemy swept up colors, guns and prisoners, he thought the end had come.

Surely Sheridan would have to move fast or they would get him too. He moved fast, but not backward. As if by a miracle, he brought one of General Emory's divisions out of nowhere and General Upton's brigade out of somewhere, and for two hours they fought, covering the ground with good men. Upton was one of them and Sheridan yelled at him to call a stretcher and get himself into a hospital in the rear.

Sheridan rode like a demon, bareheaded, his face dripping sweat and almost black with fury. He guided the lathering Rienzi with a light hand, leaping over wounded, yelling at bewildered soldiers to turn around and fight, and at the same time making plans to straighten out the melee around him.

"You, Colonel Thomas of the Eighth Vermont!" he shouted to a young man on a sorrel horse. "We must recapture those woods. Go in and do it."

"Yes, sir!" Thomas faced his men and held his sword high. "Remember Ethan Allen, boys! Come on, old Vermont!" His voice carried across the field.

He wheeled and rode at a walk toward the enemy line, which was in a woodland beyond a meadow. His veterans followed, yelling. Sheridan liked the way he did it and paused to watch. Suddenly he waved his hat and shouted, "Look there, O'Shay!" At the same moment Rick saw

Ocean Pond leap from his horse in a fringe of bushes, snatch up a fallen musket and run after the Vermonters. A smile spread over Sheridan's grim face and he chuckled, "He's following Justin Morgan, not Ethan Allen."

Eventually it would be shown that the Vermonters did recapture the wood, but no one was sure of it at the time. Sheridan's staff was furiously busy, helping reorganize the wavering front, and his aides were rounding up stragglers and strays by the hundreds, sometimes lambasting them with the flats of swords. All day the general rode alone, trailed by Rick and the flag. He and his big black horse seemed indestructible; they had been on the jump since before midnight and were still plunging in where things were hottest.

Rick had changed horses twice and several times Sheridan had ordered him to get himself coffee from field hospitals. He had obeyed only once, because those hospitals were places of horror. Losses were enormous, especially among officers. General Russell was already dead and Generals McIntosh, Chapman and Upton seriously wounded. Upton refused to go to the rear and led his men for the rest of the day on a stretcher. The Confederates were no better off and when a field changed hands the Blue and Gray lay like leaves fallen from the same tree. Stretcher-bearers and doctors paid no attention to the color of the uniforms.

It was now late in the afternoon and clouds of battle-smoke rose against the sunset and drifted away over the tortured autumn fields. Rick knew the Union line was a

crescent five miles long and, at last, it began to roll. There
was an indescribable roar of sound from big guns, little guns,
galloping horses and yelling men. It had been a long time
since a Federal army had felt victory was there to take and
gone to meet it. But it was going now. Every soldier knew
this was what he had dreamed about when he enlisted, but
had seen so seldom or never.

This was the wild, beautiful glamour of battle: long lines
of infantry stepping faultlessly, rifles shining, flags slanting
ahead, artillery belching fire and smoke, and cavalry —
there should be cavalry somewhere. There it was! Two miles
away, across a shallow valley, two divisions of blue horsemen
in solid columns were thundering down, waving their sabers
that flashed and seemed to crackle in the light. Confederate
artillery was good and its infantry was better, but neither
could stop those wild riders. They hit the Rebel line and it
crumbled. The troopers scooped up the fragments — guns,
flags, prisoners — and galloped on.

As usual, Sheridan was there to see the most dramatic act.
He came out on the brow of a hill that was held by Thomas
and his Vermonters and watched his pet cavalry division de-
liver the blow. Standing in his stirrups, he waved his hat and
cheered, and the men yelled wildly as they went forward.
Rick thought he saw Ocean with them, but he was not sure.

After that it was pandemonium in the twilight. Everywhere Early's army was in retreat and in some places in actual
rout. Discouraged Confederates were surrendering and being
marched back through fields and woods littered with the

wreckage. Much of it was human. There was not a fence corner or rock or roadside ditch where men were not dead or broken.

There was no rest. While stretcher-bearers worked by lantern light the pitiless Union cavalry pounded away, urged on by a tireless man on a tireless horse. In the darkness Jubal Early, outnumbered and defeated, but still the soldier of better days, fought to save — and did save — much of his army.

Day after day Sheridan pressed on. "Hurry up! Keep at them! Don't let them rest!" he urged his men. Telegrams of congratulation from all over the North deluged headquarters, but he had no time to read them. President Lincoln thought of coming down to thank him personally, but there is nothing to show that the general encouraged him. There wasn't time. Right now, this very minute as the dust rose from Rienzi's hoofs, the war was being won and that was all that mattered.

For the first time in a long while, the soldiers were sure of victory, and Sheridan used this new spirit to the utmost. The iron was hot and he struck again and again, smashing the enemy in several minor engagements and in one considerable battle at Fisher's Hill. At long last, the Yanks were tasting the sweets of victory.

There was also a bitterness that no one liked. As they advanced they continued the destruction of the Valley. The autumn haze thickened to a pall of smoke that stretched to the horizon as barns and stacks by the thousand in that granary of the Confederacy roared and crackled day and night. Guerrillas struck quickly and disappeared, leaving Union troopers swinging from trees. Infuriated, Sheridan ordered retaliation on civilians suspected of harboring the outlaws. He relented for he could not make war that way. But when a guerrilla was caught he was given no trial and was left swinging by the roadside. Refugees packed the highways, and the commander watched gloomily as they plodded across the desolate land. The North was ringing with his praise, the South was cursing him, and in his heart he was trying to strike a just balance.

"O'Shay," he said suddenly one day, "you have developed amazingly in six months. You are a man."

"Why — thank you, sir."

"You have matured with this army. What do you think of it?"

"It is the best on earth, sir."

"And what do you think of its commander?"

"Why . . ." Rick didn't know what to say.

"Don't answer that one." Sheridan laughed. "Faith, I can't answer it myself. But time can. Time tests a man or an army impartially." His voice trailed off, as it sometimes did when he was half talking to himself. "I am waiting for that test."

He could not have known that it would come to him and to the Army of the Shenandoah within a few days.

☆ 15 ☆

Rick lay full length in the sun, feeling delightfully lazy and contented. He had learned to grab those moments of relaxation and make the most of them. As General Sheridan had said, he had matured amazingly since spring. In this trim, well-poised lieutenant, Judge Meader would not recognize the gawky lad who had come down from the farm. War did things to a fellow and all the things it did were not bad. Even men who had been in it for years were not necessarily callous.

There was Ocean Pond, for example. Rick had given up trying to figure him out. Everything he did was so contradictory. He was too old to be in the service, yet it was impossible to think of him as anything but young. On occasion he seemed a man of the world and again he spoke like a backwoodsman. He hated war but he loved a fight. He was only a private and there was never any talk of his being promoted, yet the general treated him as an equal. In only one matter was he beyond question — his love of horses.

"Oh, hum." Rick yawned and sat up, blinking at Ocean, who sat on his heels reading a newspaper. "It seems good not to have the air full of smoke."

"Um," Ocean commented.

"I know the Valley had to be cleaned out, but I hope I never take part in such a job again."

"Um."

"The general is a hero and Mr. Lincoln will be re-elected next month, so they say, but it was a big price to pay."

"Um."

"Can't you say anything but 'Um'?"

"It is a perfectly safe sound to make." Ocean folded the paper. "A sneeze or a hiccough may be misunderstood, but never an 'Um'. When in doubt always say 'Um'."

"Come on, Ocean, what's on your mind?"

"That gang in Washington." Ocean blew angrily through his nose. "They think Jubal Early is licked and they're trying to force Sheridan to pull out of the Valley and move against Richmond from the west. They're fools, Rick, blamed fools."

"It won't be the first time, in your opinion."

"If those desk soldiers had been in the field, as we have been, they'd know Early still has a good army within a few miles of us and he knows how to use it. Give him a chance and thousands will die for no reason at all."

"Well, we can't help it." Rick shrugged.

Ocean stood up and kicked a bunch of grass viciously. "If this nation is to survive it must stop bleeding. No one will win unless this slaughter stops. That's why Sheridan is sending a flood of telegrams to Grant and the War Department begging them not to underestimate Early and give him time to strike us again." Ocean's mouth was twisting with emotion.

"I guess the general can handle things."

"He and Grant agree, sure. Sheridan is well-nigh distracted. He wants to go up there and raise the roof, but he thinks he should stay with his army."

"As far as I can see," Rick said knowingly, "we are in a good position here at Cedar Creek."

"We look strong enough on the map, sure. Maps are made of paper, but the Johnnies aren't. Early has fifteen thousand desperate men and he is receiving reinforcements. He can strike an awful blow."

They heard a horse coming at a gallop and then Captain Mike Sheridan appeared. "Pack your kit, Ocean," he said. "We're off to Washington."

"Yes, sir."

"The horses travel on the same train, that's where you come in. The general feels he may need Rienzi in an emergency."

"Considering all the jackasses there are in Washington, a good horse might come in handy."

"The general didn't *say* that." Mike laughed and cantered away.

That was October sixteenth. The seventeenth and eighteenth were quiet along the Cedar Creek front. Too quiet. Scouts reported that the Confederates were dug in back of the hills beyond the stream, but there was no activity. Old-timers who had lived on the frontier recalled the adage: "The time to look for Indians is when you can't see any," and wagged their heads. Most of the Army of the Shenandoah was tired and welcomed these few days of rest.

It was snugly asleep during the hour before the cold, foggy dawn of the nineteenth. Shooting started on the left, probably a mere picket-line fracas, but enough to wake up everyone. They might as well start their fires and temper the chilly air with hot coffee. Suddenly the Rebel artillery opened up and their infantry came whooping and yelling through the darkness, miles from where it was supposed to be. Phil Sheridan was asleep in Winchester twenty miles away.

The attack was beautifully placed and timed to hit the Union line at its weakest spot, which was Crooks' Eighth Corps. The Confederates had crept all night, much of the way single file, up a wooded ravine and were on Crooks' back before his drowsy pickets knew what was happening. His seven cannon were swarmed under and turned around to fire point-blank at the Yankees. His seven thousand men, unable to find their arms, their officers and one another in the darkness, broke for the rear.

Meanwhile, other Rebel units had materialized in the fog, their equipment muffled in rags so effectively that not a sound had told they were coming. From one end of the line to the other the surprise was complete. There was no excuse for the Federal officers. Grim "Old Jubilee" knew that, barring a miracle, he would destroy the Army of the Shenandoah before noon.

At the first alarm Rick had found his weapons and saddled a horse. He rode toward the hill where Sheridan's headquarters were, then stopped when yells and burning tents showed the Rebels were in possession there. They were in the rear of the whole Union army. A retreat was the most that could be hoped for, a rout seemed inevitable.

Rick stopped and listened and in the bedlam he had the frightful sensation of being alone, helpless to aid or to hinder anyone, his identity as completely lost as that of a raindrop in a flood. For a while, panic had him by the throat and he fled blindly with the rest.

Shameful it was to see an army of veterans, superior in numbers and equipment, being chased by a much lesser force, magnificent though the spirit of that force was. The Yankees were just as good, if there was someone to make them think so.

Rick looked down the Valley Pike and his anger boiled. Everywhere officers were struggling not with the enemy but with their own men to make them stand and fight. Some did, especially the troopers, who slapped at the fugitives with their sabers and tried to run them down. But the soldiers dodged among the horses and kept going. They were not running now, but they walked grimly, hopelessly, toward the rear. Some were half-dressed, many had thrown away their guns, others remembered they had had no breakfast and sullenly started boiling coffee, defiant of the orders that were shouted at them. Riderless horses and driverless teams added to the tangle. Rick rode up to a big man who was resting against a rail fence and shouted, "Get into line and fight, you lubber!"

"Listen, little feller," the soldier said wearily, "if the sap-heads who run this shebang had been awake this wouldn't have happened. When a army is so hard up there's only one officer I've confidence in, I'm ready to quit."

"Who do you mean?"

"Phil Sheridan, pretty likely. The minute he turns his back the whole thing goes to pot, because there isn't another gen'ral capable of taking over. That's why I'm not fighting today." He heaved himself off the fence and walked away as fresh firing broke out in the opposite direction.

Rick galloped that way and saw a Connecticut regiment making a stand around General Wright, who commanded the Sixth Corps. Wright was bareheaded and bleeding as he tried to keep his men near the Pike to block a Rebel charge. Rick joined in and for a while the line held. Then, just as the sun came up, more Confederates poured around the left end and the Connecticut men ran for their lives.

A bullet knocked Rick's hat off. Because he did not know what to do next, he recovered it and dusted it carefully, fingering the hole in the crown. Then he noticed that a force of Federals, as much as a whole brigade, was marching up the Pike to meet a larger unit of Confederates. He galloped over and pitched in, joining the Eighth Vermont Regiment, as the two columns met head on. The fury of battle was upon them. Every man was yelling and every face was distorted with rage as they went at each other with bayonets and clubbed muskets. Each stand of colors was a focal point for violence. Flags stood unsteadily in the smoke and dust. When one went down soldiers fought like demons to possess it, all thought of personal danger forgotten in the mad lust to buy pieces of silk with human lives. When a banner rose again its defenders screamed triumphantly, no matter what the blood cost had been.

Rick was as wild as any of them. Riding into the melee, he emptied his revolver, then struck out with his saber. The flag of the Vermont regiment pitched toward him and he caught it in his arms. A flash of memory recalled Colonel Thomas at Winchester and he bellowed, "Remember Ethan Allen! Come on, old Vermont!" Then, as though prompted by Ocean Pond, he added, "Come on, Justin Morgan!"

He stood in his stirrups, waving the big flag with both hands. The Confederates pressed in a half circle to beat him down and the Yankees completed the ring, protecting him with muskets, sabers and fists. Smoke-blackened faces, streaming sweat, twisted convulsively, and throats dry with dust and yelling screamed curses. A long-haired Rebel, who looked fanatical, crawled through the crowd and slashed the horse's windpipe with a bowie knife, going down the next moment under the butt of a Yankee musket. The horse reared, cascading blood, and pitched headlong. Rick jumped and they closed over him.

His next thought was that the flagstaff had cracked his head and he reached out to grab it. But it was gone — even the battle was gone. He looked at the sky, conscious of a thumping headache, then raised himself on his hands and sat up. The fight had swept on, leaving the road strewn with debris. There was heavy firing to the south so he knew his side was still retreating. Close by was the body of the horse he had been riding. Around it were seven soldiers, dead or unconscious, so torn and battered it was hard to distinguish their uniforms. A Rebel, unable to stand up, sat beside the road putting a tourniquet on a Yankee's leg. Both were talking in low, friendly tones. They broke off and watched Rick get slowly to his feet.

"You-all were lucky to get your head cracked," the Johnny said, with a slow grin.

"Lucky?" Rick rubbed his head gingerly. "Yes, it could be worse. Where is the battle?"

"Yonder." The Rebel nodded up the Pike. "It isn't a battle, it's a footrace."

"When we get squared round, we'll knock you into a cocked hat," the wounded Yank declared.

"That isn't what old Jube Early thinks."

"Did the Vermonters keep their flag?" Rick asked.

"Sure we kept it," the Yankee said. "We didn't lug it all the way from home just to give it to a damn Reb."

"Set easy, brother," the Southerner said gently. "Riling makes you bleed more."

"Hang on for a while and an ambulance will pick you fellows up," Rick promised cheerfully.

"I surely hope it's a Yank wagon," the Confederate said earnestly. "We haven't any chloroform for operations."

"We need water," the Federal said to Rick.

"I'll look around." Rick examined the fallen men and found two canteens partly full. "One for each of you."

"Obliged, Yank." The Southerner accepted his with a bow. "You-all aren't so bad."

"We've been telling you that for years," the wounded Federal said.

"It takes a war to l'arn some folks."

"Don't waste your strength gabbing," Rick advised. He went down the road to a horse whose bridle reins were caught in a smashed gun carriage. "Keep your heads up," he called back when he was mounted. Both waved to him.

Rick rode across the barren autumn fields, too bewildered to know which way to turn. His Union cavalry mount was comparatively fresh. Where could he be used to the best advantage? The firing was still heavy, proving that many Yankees were still hanging on, but they had retreated so fast they must be at least four miles from where they started. The litter of defeat reached as far as Rick could see: equipment of all kinds wrecked or thrown away, dead and wounded where the lines had met, walking wounded, and plenty walking who were not wounded. Except for the distant voice of the guns, the dull silence of despair was everywhere.

And then came Sheridan.

Rick saw him sweep over a low hill and come pounding down the other side, the great black horse galloping with powerful ease. His staff and a few dozen troopers trailed in a cloud of gray dust.

"It's Sheridan!" The shout went up from a group of men boiling coffee in a grove.

The general pulled up and waved his hat madly. "Turn around, boys!" he yelled. "We'll give them the worst licking they ever had. Turn around! Come on!" He was off.

The soldiers threw their caps in the air and forgot their coffee. They scattered, waving their rifles over their heads and whooping to men across the fields, "That was Sheridan! Come on!" Because there was magic in the man, they turned and followed him — soldiers, teamsters, even noncombatant hangers-on. Suddenly everyone felt rested and gay, sure beyond a doubt that things were all right.

Rick joined the cavalcade, coming in diagonally behind Mike and Major Forsyth, who were spurring their jaded horses.

"Mine eyes have seen the glory of the coming of the Lord," a high-pitched voice chanted, and Ocean came up on a dapple-gray, black with sweat.

"Whoop-whoop-whoopeeeee!" Rick waved a fist over his head. "We've got a twist on them now!"

"Isn't he wonderful!" Ocean shouted.

"The greatest soldier on earth!"

"I mean Rienzi. Twenty miles and fresh as a daisy. Didn't I tell you Justin Morgan was created to win this war!"

The horse galloped on, nostrils wide, eyes on fire, sharing the spirit of his rider. Everywhere the battered Union army felt their presence. Miles away the words, "Sheridan has come!" stopped men in their tracks, turned them around and sent them back cheering. Soldiers, defeated hours before, who had thrown away their weapons and slunk off, were now forming lines and cheering as though the battle had been won.

Finally Sheridan reached the front. The Sixth Corps was still a unit and its commander, General Wright, was still fighting, though so weak from loss of blood he lay on the ground as he gave his orders. Sheridan rode along the line and the corps exploded in one mighty cheer.

"We'll lick them, boys!" he shouted. "Before night we will give Jubal Early the worst licking he ever had."

It was not an empty promise. He took his time welding the fragments of his broken army and he did a masterly job. It was past midafternoon when he gave the order to advance. Every man in the Army of the Shenandoah knew this was it. Early and his splendid troops were good as ever, but they were not good enough now. They broke, rallied, broke again and poured back the way they had come, back past the Federal camp of the morning, and still back. The cavalry plowed into the mob, through and over the wagon trains and artillery, sweeping up all the guns and vehicles they had lost early in the day, together with twenty-five Rebel cannon, stands of colors by the dozen and uncounted prisoners. When darkness came Jubal Early's army was done for.

Phil Sheridan rode slowly past a great fire some of the men had kindled. As they watched him, they realized they were tasting glory with the little man and the great horse.

☆ 16 ☆

CORRESPONDENTS ASSIGNED TO THE ARMY OF THE SHENAN-doah marveled at the way General Sheridan mixed with his men. There was no condescension about it, he was one of them. He was the hero of the hour. Grant ordered one hundred gun salutes fired in his honor by every battery at Petersburg, Lincoln promoted him to major general in the Regular Army, the North idolized him, yet Sheridan was not spoiled. His headquarters was still one tent for himself and another for his small staff, with no display of sentries or banners. He demanded the respect due his position, but he never acted, because he never felt, as though he were made of better stuff than the men who served under him.

Officially, they served under him, but every one of them was serving with him. So fantastic was his energy that almost everyone in the army caught sight of him every day. Riding at a gallop on the horse that was already legendary, he showed up everywhere. On night marches they heard his voice in the darkness; if there was a traffic jam they knew he would soon be there to straighten it out; he would eat their food and blow the commissary sky-high if it was not good. He would tiptoe through a hospital tent, his swarthy, weather-beaten face softened by compassion; and when battle came he was in the thick of it, seeing it all, roaring his orders, cursing laggards, gesturing madly with his little hat, jumping the wild-eyed, bare-toothed horse over the breastworks with never a scratch on either of them, as if they were one and inviolate in their fury.

George Townshend of the New York *Herald* was doing an article about Rienzi and had gone over to the campfire where Ocean, Rick and Mike Sheridan were talking shop.

"Then, as I understand it, Pond, this horse won the battle of Cedar Creek by carrying his master at a gallop all those twenty miles," he summarized.

"Use your head more and your imagination less, young man," Ocean said bluntly. "No horse, not even Rienzi, could go belly-to-the-ground for twenty miles. I was there. Most of the time we trotted and some of the time we walked and now and then we stopped altogether. But, mister," his voice rose a pitch, "there were times when the rest of us couldn't keep within gunshot of that black streak. It reminded me of the dinner bell on my grandfather's woodshed."

"Yes," Townshend asked, after a full minute of silence, "what about the bell?"

"Oh, the bell? It used to flop back and forth in the wind. One day during a big thunderstorm it got to going so fast that Grandfather said he saw the lightning strike at it seven times and miss."

"And you are the one who just criticized me for using my imagination!" The reporter laughed with the others.

Mike leaned forward on his elbows. "Joking aside," he said, "I never saw a horse that could run like Rienzi."

"You feel that he won the battle?" Townshend persisted.

"Ocean does." Mike winked at Rick.

"I don't," Ocean said flatly. "It was won by Justin Morgan." And he gave Townshend his version of the divine creation of the first Morgan horse, whose destiny was to save the Union by providing Rienzi for General Sheridan.

"An exceedingly interesting thought," Townshend said. "May I use it in the *Herald*?"

"Sure." Ocean stood up. "Tell your paper the war was won by Rienzi through old Justin."

"But the war isn't won yet," Townshend reminded him.

"Listen." It was hard to believe that Ocean, who was known as a joker, could be so serious. "The war was won at Cedar Creek. It showed the whole Union, and the Rebels too, there will be no more talk about peace without victory. Abraham Lincoln will be elected on that."

"Quite possibly, Mr. Pond, but even that may not end the war."

"If you are as intelligent as I think you are, Mr. Townshend, you know that if the Confederacy had won that battle it might have led to the collapse of the United States. Then there would be no truly democratic government on earth." Ocean turned on his heel and walked into the darkness.

"He seems to be dedicated to glorifying the Morgan horse," Townshend said thoughtfully.

"He is," Rick agreed. "Of course, he carries it too far

sometimes. There is good reason to believe it was not a horse but a man named Sheridan who won the battle of Cedar Creek."

"I am getting too much credit for that." Sheridan walked into the firelight, holding his meershaum pipe in one hand. "Anyone got a match?"

"Here, sir." Townshend jumped to oblige.

"Thank you." Sheridan lighted his pipe. "Too much credit," he repeated. "It is a fine army, officers and men, and it would have pulled itself together without me."

"But it would not have cleaned up the Valley as you have done, sir. You may be proud of that," Townshend said with conviction.

"I wonder." The general started pacing back and forth, for he never could keep still. "Grant ordered it. It was necessary to destroy Lee's source of supply. But I wonder. Those barns. Those beautiful cattle. Those rich farms. I am a country boy, Townshend. I love such things and I know how hard those good people worked to get them."

"That is war, sir."

"Do you think I enjoy death and destruction? Do you think I am happy to bring misery upon people? And my boys! Two thousand were killed. Many more will die of wounds. And there were perhaps as many more fine, young Confederates. Do you think, Mr. Townshend, I won a glorious victory?"

"Yes, General, I do, inasmuch as the war could not be won by any other means."

"You may be right. I hope you are right. I pray Almighty

God this killing may stop. But until it does stop, I must go on. Good night, gentlemen."

He must go on and he did go on. He sent most of the infantry and artillery to join Grant at the siege of Petersburg and with the cavalry went into winter quarters around Kernstown. It was officially called winter quarters, but little hibernating was done there. The guerrillas were more troublesome and the way they pillaged and murdered made Sheridan decide to deal with them once and for all. They were concentrated in Loudoun County, where many of the inhabitants were giving them shelter. That was where he blasted them. Private dwellings and the property of Quakers were spared, everything else was destroyed on the spot or carried off. The outlaws received in full measure what was coming to them.

When the job was done and an exact account rendered there and elsewhere in the once-lovely Shenandoah Valley, Sheridan grimly added up the total: 3772 horses, 545 mules, 10,918 cattle, 12,000 sheep, 15,000 hogs, 250 calves, 71 flour mills, 1 woolen mill, 8 sawmills, 1 powder mill, 3 saltpeter works, 1200 barns, 7 furnaces, 4 tanneries, 1 railroad depot, 435,802 bushels of wheat, 20,000 bushels of oats, 77,176 bushels of corn, 874 barrels of flour, 20,397 tons of hay, 500 tons of fodder, 450 tons of straw, 12,000 pounds of bacon, 10,000 pounds of tobacco, 2500 bushels of potatoes, 1665 pounds of cotton yarn. The double task of driving out the guerrillas and emptying General Lee's storehouse had been accomplished. Now for Lee himself.

The weather was severe that winter, with snow on the

heights and mud, mud, mud in the Valley. Ocean worked mightily on Rienzi but the horse was seldom clean, for Sheridan went splashing around day and night. With the approach of spring Sheridan's work was done there and he led his troopers up the Pike. At the south end, near Waynesboro, he stopped to dispose of the last pitiful remnant of Early's army, picking up about sixteen hundred prisoners, eleven guns, two hundred loaded wagons and some twenty battle flags. Then he slogged down to Petersburg, which was the most hopeless spot either side had ever fought in.

The stalemate had held for months and months. Disease had taken a terrible toll and the Army of the Potomac was mud-soaked in body and spirit. But when it saw Phil Sheridan ride in with his ten thousand horsemen, bands playing, flags snapping in the wind, it got a lift the like of which it had not known. Here was an army that was actually victorious. Here was a general who won battles. Here was hope. Before their eyes, as they yelled their heads off, rode the bandy-legged little hero everyone talked about. He was the man they honestly believed could take them out of the mud and out of the doldrums and out of the war in the good old Yankee way. Grant and Meade were around somewhere, but they were colorless that day.

General Sheridan was pleased with his reception. He knew Grant's problems were far greater than his own and that the silent, stoop-shouldered man had done wonders in his dogged, unspectacular way. There was an understanding and respect between the two that was fine to see. Jealousy had no place there for they were dedicated to the task of winning the war rather than to jockeying for personal gain. Compared with his quicksilver junior, Grant was a ponderous thinker. Each had bulldog tenacity and the ability to see beyond the horizon. They were a rare team.

Robert E. Lee was better than either of them, as everyone knew. With equal resources, he would have settled things long ago, before the North woke up. Now, with his depleted army in rags, half his horses demobilized from lack of fodder and no replacements to hope for, he was holding Petersburg, on the outskirts of the Confederate capital, in spite of all the mighty Army of the Potomac could do.

That army had done a prodigious amount of work there, as Sheridan's men realized when they saw the place. City Point, on the James River, was now a great port with more than a mile of docks along its banks. Any day the wondering inland Yanks could see forty steamboats, twice as many sailing craft and innumerable barges tied up there. There were immense warehouses, blacksmith shops, bakeries, army barracks and quarters for civilian employees. A hospital for ten thousand patients covered two hundred acres. Water was pumped to this city and sprinkling carts laid the dust in the streets. A twenty-one-mile railroad, complete with yards, shops and docks, had been built from the river to the Petersburg trenches. On the Confederate side such facilities, less extensive, were supplied by the city of Richmond.

The trench systems of the two armies were as fantastic and depressing as a bad dream. They twisted and turned for thirty-five miles, studded with forts and faced with masses of tangled treetops and rows of sharpened stakes, with rifle pits reaching out toward each other. In the rear were woods, gradually disappearing for fuel, and among the stumps were cities of tents and huts. Everywhere there was mud, desolate, heartsickening mud that soaked the soldiers' clothing, mildewed their blankets, rusted their equipment, and got into their food. Malaria, pneumonia, and trench fever thrived in it, countless feet and an endless rain of bullets, shells and bombs churned it to a bloody goo. It stank, it crawled with vermin, it had every discomfort and not one virtue.

This had been going on since June and it was now March. The hateful mud had created a bond of sympathy on both sides so that Yanks and Rebs rarely aimed deliberately at each other. When they had to shoot to keep up appearances they yelled a warning and if the officers objected to that the men quietly sighted their guns at a harmless angle. At night the pickets got together and talked and played cards and swapped this for that. It did not mean they would not fight as fiercely as ever when there was worthwhile fighting to do. They agreed it was silly to be kept on edge by piddling scraps that couldn't possibly affect the war one way or another. It was better to enjoy themselves as much as possible until something began to give.

As the men in the trenches looked at it, this business

might go on for years. Being almost one of Sheridan's official family, Rick knew the top Federal officers thought differently. He overheard or was told enough to know that Grant was constantly inching to the southwest, trying to get around Lee's right and cut the railroads that supplied his army and Richmond. To block Grant, Lee was obliged to reach farther and farther and stretch his thin line thinner. Eventually, despite his genius and the heroism of the Confederacy, the line would break.

Sheridan had not been in the Petersburg area a day before he longed for action. Much as he admired Grant's tenacity, he could not abide the stalemate. He believed, with good reason, that the sodden Army of the Potomac was low on morale and might get stale if not allowed to fight before long.

"Let me go," Rick heard him urge Grant, as the officers paced up and down in a rainstorm that had continued for days. "I know I can get around Lee and grab the railroad. I know I can! Then he will be forced into the open where we can finish him. Let me go!"

"You can't move in this mud," Grant said gloomily.

"Yes, I can, if I have to corduroy every foot of the roads." Sheridan drove one fist into his palm. "I know I can!"

They went into Grant's tent together and Rick heard no more.

A few days later it was noised around headquarters that Grant, after a long talk with President Lincoln and General Sherman, had decided the time had come. The success of the operation would depend on Sheridan's ability to destroy the railroad in Lee's rear, while the rest of the Union army came out of the hated trenches and hit Petersburg. It might mean the end of the war.

"If you can pray, pray now, Rick," Ocean said on the evening of March twenty-eight. "We're off in the morning."

"A lot of us are praying tonight," Rick answered.

☆ 17 ☆

It was three o'clock the next morning when the army moved out. The clouds were low and a chill rose from the soggy earth. The cavalry went first, nearly ten thousand troopers walking their horses slowly, as they always did when there was serious business ahead. The men talked in low tones, for they had learned long ago that going into battle was not the gay adventure it is supposed to be. Some said they thought this was the beginning of the end and others warned them there was still plenty of ginger left in the Johnnies. They had great respect for the Confederates and hoped they would not be obliged to kill many more of them.

And they talked about the object and plans for this move, for as usual, the men in the ranks managed to know what was going on. It was pretty well understood that the Old Man was using General Ord's three divisions and a couple of extra corps to keep the Rebels busy at Petersburg. Meanwhile he was sending General Humphreys and the Second Corps, General Warren and the Fifth Corps, and Sheridan with his three mounted divisions to turn Lee's flank, cut the railroad in his rear and force him from the trenches into the open.

Grant entrusted Sheridan with this flanking attempt and issued orders that he was to be in command of it, a fact that didn't sit well with Warren. He was a good officer, a genuine hero at Gettysburg, but he was tired now and unable to meet the demands of the younger and indefatigable Sheridan.

Daylight found the cavalry plugging along grimly. Spring might be in the air but so was fog and a cold wind. The countryside was monotonous, a level stretch of second-growth timber and brush, cut in every direction by sluggish little streams that went nowhere. Rick hated it and hated more the miserable little side roads he was forever traveling with messages to and from the infantry that was advancing on the right toward a nothing-at-all called Hatcher's Run. He wondered where Hatcher ran and what he would find when he reached there.

Toward noon Rick overtook Ocean walking beside a blacksmith's wheeled forge, leading his horse.

"Nice sugaring weather," Rick shouted, for he had been thinking of home.

"You never saw any real maple sugar in York State," Ocean scoffed.

"We make lots of it there."

"Lots of something. Maple sugar comes only from Vermont."

"Along with Justin Morgan."

"They say Justin didn't dare eat sugar — it gave him too much energy. He tried it once in a race and they couldn't stop him for twelve days. Wouldn't have stopped him then if he hadn't worn the track so deep in the ground he struck water and got stuck in the mud."

"Don't mention mud. I can see too much of it."

"There'll be more rain, my corns sting."

"Then why don't you ride?"

"It's too uncomfortable. I'm only happy when I'm uncomfortable because I'm happy when I get over it."

"Is that feller cracked?" a soldier asked, as Rick rode past.

"No, he's perfectly normal because he's different."

Ocean spoke as a prophet. It began to rain that evening as the cavalry camped at a wretched crossroads named Dinwiddie Courthouse because a courthouse was actually there. The men spent a dreary and profane night, tents leaked, blankets were wet, provisions were waterlogged, fires wouldn't burn. The only cheering thought was that the enemy was no better off.

Rick shivered in his dog tent, yet a year in the army had taught him to stand on his own feet and not be afraid. If he survived the war his pockets would be empty, but he had a fund of self-reliance no amount of money could buy.

The rain did not let up. When daylight came, the whole area looked like, and was, a swamp. All the innumerable little streams were over their banks and water stood on the roads, fields and woodlands. Sheridan scorned the weather and sent Rienzi plowing through the mud to inspection of troop positions. He found the infantry bogged down at Hatcher's Run, where the most optimistic officers doubted the possibility of staying on top of the ground, let alone trying to advance. If a horse stood in one place for a few minutes it sank to its belly and had to be pulled out by soldiers. Even Rienzi could travel only at a walk.

Grant had moved his headquarters over to Gravelly Run and was trying to decide what to do. When he asked the advice of his staff, he was told that the most to be hoped for was to hang on until the weather cleared. He was no quitter, but the rain was coming down so hard that he finally gave orders to abandon all thought of advancing at present.

Then Sheridan splashed up, dripping ooze to the crown of his once-black hat. This was no time to stop, he told the amazed officers. It was a grand opportunity to hit the Confederates, who were worse off than the Union army.

"Can you advance?" Grant's chief of staff, John Rawlins, asked incredulously.

"Of course I can!" Sheridan slapped his hands together.

Rawlins moved a step to avoid sinking in the mud and asked, "How, sir?"

"How?" Sheridan shouted. "If I have to, I will put every one of my men to corduroying the roads. There is plenty of timber. I will corduroy every foot of the way from Dinwiddie to the railroad."

"I believe he could do it, sir!" Rawlins said to Grant, suddenly on fire with hope. "I know he could!"

Grant gave the little general a long, searching look, then asked quietly, "When will you be ready to move, Sheridan?"

"Tomorrow." There was no question of doubt. "Tomorrow I can go to smashing things."

"Go at it." Grant calmly flicked the ash from his cigar. "And don't stop until the job is finished."

Sheridan went at it as only he knew how to do. The rain continued, but every drop of it was a challenge to him. And somehow, in that magic way of his, he put the fire of heroism in the hearts of his men. Custer's entire division, famous for the punch it packed, was given the heartbreaking job of corduroying the road to the rear, over which the supply trains must come up. Thousands of axes cut tens of thousands of trees and laid them in the mud. The men cursed the weather, but not their orders, and they joked about the gunboats and Noah's ark that would soon show up. By late afternoon the wagons came floundering in.

That night the rain was as mean as ever. The troopers regarded it as a personal enemy and resolved to fight it until it had nothing left to throw at them. They slept on brush piles or propped up against stumps, and the wagons moved all night. Sheridan encouraged and directed, sometimes got down to put a shoulder to a wheel. His familiar "Hurry up!" was not heard because he knew they were doing their utmost.

"Where did you sleep?" Rick asked Ocean in the morning.

"In a bed softer than feathers."

"Yes, you did!"

"Sure, in mud. I didn't move till daylight, when a mule team pulled me out."

Custer and his men were at it early. There was mud in

the general's long yellow curls and his resplendent uniform was ruined, but he was not complaining. He always liked to accomplish the impossible. They worked all the forenoon, and the long lines of forage, food and ammunition moved faster and faster. Sheridan left a division to hold the court-house and moved north to "start smashing things," as he had promised Grant.

It had been impossible to do much scouting. He did not know the Confederates were dug in a few miles up the road at a hamlet called Five Forks. He soon found out. Behind the breastworks was practically all the cavalry Lee had left and five grim infantry divisions under General Pickett of Gettysburg fame. They were ready for a desperate stand there in the mud and rain, for if the crossroads fell the rail-road in the rear would be cut and Petersburg and Richmond lost.

Sheridan realized the stakes and, though he had only one division under General Devin on hand, he did not hesitate. Ordering the troopers to dismount and do the best they could, he raced back to Dinwiddie Courthouse to put the others in line. There was no time to write orders or consult staff officers. "Mike," he roared, "find Custer and tell him to get up here quick! O'Shay, locate every gun you can and tell 'em I want 'em at the courthouse." He was off, bare-headed and fiery-eyed, Rienzi's hoofs throwing mud to the treetops.

Devin was fighting hard up front, but he was heavily out-numbered and falling back. It was an orderly withdrawal.

Behind the line was confusion and disorder where each of a thousand cavalrymen was trying to manage three horses besides his own. Mud tried to pull them down, trees and fences tried to tangle them up, Rebel bullets tried to pick them off, but most of the kicking, squealing, yelling mix-up finally got back to the crossroads.

Sheridan got his three divisions more or less where he wanted them and then he did something even the spectacle-loving Custer would not have thought of: he ordered all the regimental bands to the front and told them to play — to play as loud and fast as they could and keep it up until they were told to stop. It was as though he was so sure of victory he had already begun the celebration. The music raised the spirits of those dog-weary men and they waved their caps and cheered. Just then the evening sun came out and the entire Confederate force moved forward.

Sheridan galloped the length of the line with, as many a soldier declared, forked lightning shooting from his eyes. The Rebels threw in everything they had, which was much, but the line held. Then darkness came and the Confederates drew back out of range. Fires twinkled on both sides and lanterns moved back and forth as the stretcher parties went to work.

"It looks as though we're outnumbered two to one." Rick was lying on a blanket too tired to eat for a while.

"Stand still, you ornery hoss." Ocean was trying to comb the mud out of Rienzi's tail. "There's so much band music mixed with this clay that when it dries out you'll probably sneeze to the tune of *Yankee Doodle*." He turned to Rick. "Our infantry will be here before morning. Warren's corps is only six miles away."

"The general is getting sick of the way Warren drags his feet. I heard him tell Grant the other day he wished he had Wright's Sixth Corps instead of Warren's Fifth."

"You shouldn't eavesdrop on your superiors, boy."

"I didn't eavesdrop. When Sheridan gets excited you can hear him a mile."

Sheridan was in a blistering rage when Warren had not appeared at dawn. Mike, who was not afraid of his brother, tried to reason with him, pointing out that the Fifth Corps had fought nearly all the day before with some of Lee's infantry, and then floundered all night through swamps. No wonder they were late. That made no difference to Phil Sheridan. Because Warren had not shown up on time, the Rebels had pulled back to their earthworks and Five Forks and a great opportunity had been lost. Warren was a lazy so-and-so and always had been, which Mike denied because Warren was one of the best generals, though a bit over-cautious at times.

"All right, all right, all right!" Sheridan stamped up and down in the mud. "But if it happens again I'll break him if it's the last thing I ever do."

It was noon before the Fifth Corps reached Dinwiddie Courthouse. They were pitifully tired after their terrific twenty-four hours, but Sheridan let them rest only an hour or two. He had found a hole between the Confederate in-

fantry and cavalry, and knew if he could take advantage of
it the whole war might collapse. That was an immediate
possibility now — to win not only the battle but the war. It
was of such tremendous importance that nothing, absolutely
nothing else mattered.

Sheridan threw himself into preparations for the battle
with the fury of a madman, though every move counted. He
was everywhere, directing, prodding, cursing, gesturing.
Staid officers of the old school — Warren was one — secretly
scorned his lack of poise, but the men loved it. As on the day
before, the mounted bands, which used to have an easy time,
were put well up in front and ordered to play their heads off.
At four o'clock ten thousand cavalry and sixteen thousand
infantry were moving toward the enemy lines.

Rick again carried the general's flag, the little swallowtail
one with the stars, and tried to keep up with Rienzi. Sheridan was acting intuitively, for things moved too fast to be
analyzed. He knew, though in the smoky woods he could
not have seen, that Warren had blundered again and was
leading his three divisions so far east they would miss the
Confederates altogether. Warren himself was actually lost
and for some time could not be located by his own staff. It
looked as though there was a wide-open hole in the Federal,
not the Rebel, line. The brilliant Pickett would surely find
it. Sheridan galloped into the woods and appeared to swing
the line around by main force.

"Come on, come on, come on! Give it to 'em, boys! You
can lick 'em! Follow me!" he shouted. A soldier pitched

headlong and a comrade bent over him. "Don't stop now!" Sheridan waved him on. "We'll pick him up later. Every minute counts now."

"For God's sake, sir, get out of here!" General Chamberlain shouted. "You are too valuable, sir. We will carry on."

"Valuable! What is one Irishman more or less?" Sheridan laughed and rode into a hotter fight.

The battle roared on and finally Warren and most of his men were turned around so they could hit Pickett in flank and rear, though the Gray veterans were still holding magnificently.

"O'Shay!" Sheridan pulled up, his face black with battle smoke. "Give me that battle flag."

"Yes, sir!" Rick had an awful moment, wondering if he was being relieved because of some fault.

Sheridan took the flag and, waving it over his head, rode along the front and part way back. Then he trotted straight for the Rebel line and the men followed, cheering. Even the wounded on the ground threw their caps in the air. The general rose in his stirrups as Rienzi cleared the breastworks. The yelling soldiers swarmed after him. It was an irresistible force. The Confederate line crumbled and the Yankees roared on, too excited to stop to round up prisoners.

But Sheridan paused long enough to write an order to General Warren relieving him of his command and telling him to report at Grant's headquarters.

"Read it," he said to Mike, grimly.

The captain went over it carefully. "A cruel thing to do, Phil," was all he said.

"Cruel!" Sheridan's eyes blazed. "He has been slow obeying orders a dozen times. It has cost the lives of hundreds, perhaps thousands, of boys. I will have no more of it."

Before he could gather his troops for an attack on the railroad it was dark. That could be done tomorrow. The Confederate army was broken beyond repair now. Robert E. Lee knew the end was not far off. So did Grant. That night he issued orders for a general advance on Petersburg.

☆ 18 ☆

RICK SLEPT SO SOUNDLY HE DID NOT KNOW THE NIGHT SKY above Petersburg miles away was alive with fire as every gun in the hundreds of Union batteries cut loose. He was only half awake when the bugles sounded before dawn and Sheridan ordered an all-out pursuit of what was left of the Rebels who had fought at Five Forks.

The fugitives had kept on retreating during the night. It was impossible to overtake many of them. The railroad was cut, but before long that in itself was not so important, because the news spread that Petersburg had fallen and Richmond was being abandoned. At first the men would not believe it and when they were finally convinced they were not sure what it meant to them. Certainly it was a good thing to have Lee out in the open, but no one could believe he would not make a lot of trouble yet.

Sheridan was greatly excited, so Rick overheard much at headquarters and on the road, where he met and talked with officers. Lee's one chance, they said, was to scrape his survivors together and try to join General Joe Johnston's small army in North Carolina. That would make him travel south and west, and the Army of the Potomac should be able to

head him off because it had a shorter distance to go. His best
bet was to run for Amelia Courthouse and get his troops on
the train before the Yankees arrived. So the plan was not
to try to overtake him at present but to get around him and
stop him before he joined Johnston.

In other words, it became clear that Grant and Lee were
putting on a gigantic footrace. Sheridan and his cavalry were
leading the Northern team, with Grant, Meade and the infantry following as fast as they could. That was pretty fast,
for those veterans could do better than thirty-five miles a
day and keep it up. They were always good and now they
had a tremendous incentive. It was spring, the world was
green again; there were flowers beside the roads and in the
woodlands. Hope was in the air. For the first time since that
far-off spring, when war seemed glamorous and gay, there
was the promise of peace. This very summer they might
harvest the crops now being planted in the North, and the
bluebirds now nesting in New England orchards might still
be singing when the blue uniforms were put away. The road
home was this very one they were traveling, so there was an
eagerness in their steps and a length to their strides as their
hearts beat to the tempo of Phil Sheridan's battle cry:
"Hurry up-hurry up-hurry up!"

Out in front, Sheridan's superbly mounted scouts jabbed
at the Confederate rear guard, slipped away and jabbed
again, looking for a weak spot. But especially they wanted
to keep in touch with Lee's army just enough to see if the
Union turning movement was succeeding. It was, and after

two days Sheridan clattered into the small town of Jeters-
ville on the Richmond and Danville Railroad before Lee
reached there.

If he was going any farther in his race toward the south
Lee would have to fight for this railroad. In the old days he
would have made quick work of it, for he was only six miles
away at Amelia Courthouse. Now the road was too long for
his staggering horses and starving men. Like a wounded fox
he turned west, hoping to reach the Southside Railroad and
get provisions from Lynchburg. From three sides the Army
of the Potomac came on in full cry, Grant, Meade, Sheridan, Ord, Custer, and all the rest. The woods were green
with new leaves that were beginning to shade the long winding roads, but the road the Confederacy was traveling was
becoming pitifully short and straight.

"They had such beautiful horses once!" Ocean stopped
on a hill and looked down at what must have been some
officer's pride. It had the lines of a thoroughbred as it lay in
the dust, its starved body quivering in the agony of exhaustion. "The animals aren't to blame, they are driven."

"So are we driven," Rick said bitterly, "driven by something inside us. Both sides driven by the same thing, whatever it is. But the Johnnies won't drive much longer." He
looked across the fields that were hideous with wreckage:
broken wagons, splintered ambulances, guns, small arms,
blanket rolls, carcasses of horses and mules. There was
human wreckage: bodies still unburied, casualties and exhausted stragglers waiting to be picked up.

"Don't say that," Ocean told him. "When this is over both sides must drive harder than ever, but it will be for unity. The Union has been preserved and it must be maintained. We will all lose what it cost us if we don't all pull together. And we will. We are made of the same stuff."

"I hope you're right," Rick said slowly. "I can't see beyond the end of the war. If I live till then I hope to own a horse. That's the only plan I have. Not very ambitious, eh?"

"You might do worse," Ocean said.

It was no time to plan the future when the present was exploding. Nosing out in front like a hunting dog, Custer spotted a long line of Rebel wagons struggling up a hill through the woods. That was his quarry. His bugles shrieked and his horsemen came in belly-to-the-ground, flags snapping and sabers swinging. The Confederate infantry wheeled to meet the charge, but the troopers whirled around them and hit the train broadside. Horses, men and wagons were piled up in a fierce tangle, taut traces were cut and teams went plunging away. Teamsters dived under wagons only to crawl out to surrender, for the Yanks had set fire to the loads. Sheridan, coming pell-mell to see what was going on, looked down from the hilltop to find this was no mere train but a whole section of Lee's army, commanded by General Ewell, that had been cut off.

"Mike! Forsyth! O'Shay!" he roared to his nearest aides. "The Sixth Corps is over on the Pike. Tell them to get up here quick and we'll bag the whole caboodle. Quick!"

The messengers thundered off and found the Sixth Corps making camp. A hollow-eyed colonel protested to Colonel Forsyth, "We have marched all night and all day, sir, without food. Who says we can't stop to rest?"

"General Sheridan's orders, sir."

The veterans of the Valley heard the word "Sheridan" and grabbed their rifles. They cheered as they formed ranks. They got into line on the hill overlooking a creek and Sheridan galloped up.

"There are three divisions of them," he shouted in his booming battle voice. "It's Lee's whole right wing. Don't let them get away, boys! Eat them up!"

Rick saw the Blue line begin to move. For about a minute it went at a walk, both horse and foot, then it charged full tilt. The troopers of Custer, Devin and Crook hit the Gray flanks and rolled around to the rear, while the grand old Sixth Corps smashed the center. The Confederates fought like wild men, but the time had come when even their courage was not enough. Raked from end to end, front and rear, the line crumbled and would never be reformed. The Yanks swamped them and they surrendered, seven thousand on the spot and two thousand more rounded up soon afterward. One-legged General Ewell was a prisoner, a hard way to reach the end of the road he had traveled so proudly with Stonewall Jackson. With him was young Custis Lee, the commander's son. This battle of Sailor's Creek was not the end of the war, but it was the end of the Confederacy's hope.

Both armies camped by the creek that night, the prisoners roped off but free to move about. Few of them cared to move, for they were worn out. For four years their spirit had amazed the world, but at last they had reached a point beyond human endurance. They sat by the fires in gloomy silence, eating the abundant rations the victors pressed on them, too tired to think of anything beyond the solace of food and rest.

The Yankees were whooping it up, dancing around the fires, parading captured flags and uniforms and throwing handfuls of Confederate money around, for they had found bales of it in a wagon. But Rick was not in the mood for that. It was depressing to see the sorrow of men who had fought so long and so well. Their cause was unjust, he was sure of it, but they did not think so and had staked everything on their convictions. It was right for them to lose, but Rick would have enjoyed their defeat a lot more if he had hated them.

General Sheridan acted as though he felt the same way. He invited the Rebel generals to mess with him and then they all sat around the fire talking. Most of them were making the best of it, but Ewell, who had been one of Lee's main supports, was disconsolate and sat with his head in his hands. Up until that morning he had hoped against hope, but now he knew it was the end. In a broken voice he asked Sheridan to send a flag of truce to Lee, who was only a few miles away, and beg him to end the bloodshed. The fury of battle had left Sheridan and he replied gently that Grant was the one to do that. Then ask Grant, Ewell begged, and Sheridan went to his tent to write the request.

Rick was wandering about, thinking of another cup of coffee before turning in, when a fistfight broke out between two of the prisoners. The Yanks laughed and egged them on until a captain of the provost guard interfered.

"Don't you Johnnies have war enough without making war on your own men?" he growled, collaring both of them.

"He ain't one of us, sir," the lanky one retorted. "He's a deserter, a thievin', murderin' guerrilla."

"That's a lie," the other whimpered.

Rick spun around, for it was the voice of Ed Potts.

"Sir," the Southerner was furious but polite, "I am Eben Hawkins. You-all can find my name on the roll of the Tenth Virginia Volunteers. I come from Winchester in the Valley."

"And what if you do?" the captain snapped.

"Sir, this polecat murdered my brother and robbed his dead body. He's a guerrilla that fought on both sides and in the middle. I know, sir. I've been hunting him and I've just caught up with him. I ask you, sir, not to let him get away."

The officer motioned to a couple of aides, who snapped handcuffs on Ed's wrists.

"He's lyin', mister." As usual, Ed was ready to blubber. "I'm a United States soldier from Michigan. I've fit in more'n twenty battles, mister."

"Which ones?"

"Bull Run — Shiloh — Gettysburg." Ed hesitated.

"Lexington?" the captain prompted.

"Yes, sure, Lexin'ton."

"Waterloo?"

"Yeh, I was there too."

The bystanders shouted with laughter, and Ed grinned hopefully.

"March him over to the barn and put the leg irons on him," the captain ordered. "We're taking no chances with this bird."

Ed clasped his manacled hands for mercy and looked around for help. His eyes widened and his mouth fell open. "Rick!" he cried. "You'll save me, won't you? You'll tell 'em I'm a honest soldier."

Rick eyed him contemptuously. "Do you expect me to do that, Ed?"

The captain said, "Do you know him, Lieutenant?"

"Yes." Rick's tone implied there was nothing more to be said.

"Come along, you," one of the guards ordered.

Ed's fat face was pasty white in the firelight. "Rick, I've got to talk to you alone. I've got to tell you somethin'."

"Well, tell me."

"I've got to talk to you alone, Rick."

"There's time if you want to grant the last request of a condemned man, Lieutenant." The captain winked at Rick.

There was a small building, so fouled by the recent use of cattle that the army had no use for it. They shackled

Ed's ankles, hung a lantern on a beam and went out, posting a sentry outside the closed door.

"Now, what do you want?" Rick demanded brusquely.

"I want you to tell that officer feller that what that lousy Johnny said was a big lie." Ed's tone was almost commanding.

"You want me to say you are not a deserter, a thief, a guerrilla and a murderer?"

"Yeh, that's it. Then he'll let me go."

"Ed," Rick said distinctly, "I shall tell him the truth: you are a deserter, you are a thief, you are a guerrilla. I can't prove you are a murderer, but I know you tried hard to murder me. I haven't forgotten how that rope felt around my neck."

"I ain't askin' no favors." Ed tried to sound dignified. "I can pay. Poor Pa died last winter. Did you know that, Rick?"

"No."

"He left me th' farm, Rick, ever'thing. I'll sign it all over to you if you'll tell th' captain I'm a honest soldier."

Rick looked at him for a long moment. "You ask me to lie, to take a bribe, to violate my word as an officer, in order to save a man who never had a shred of honor to start with and has committed the Lord only knows how many crimes? No, Ed, I won't do it." He turned on his heel. As he went through the door Ed cried out something, but he did not turn around.

"Did you cheer his last moments, Lieutenant?" the captain asked, outside.

"I am afraid not, sir." Rick told parts of the story.

"It's amazing how mean a human being can be!" the captain said in disgust.

"The only possible excuse is that he never was very bright. I honestly doubt if he knows right from wrong, sir. He is too big a coward to fight his conscience."

"Are you suggesting leniency, Lieutenant?"

"Yes, sir." Rick looked over at the campfires. "I am so sick of killing, I hate to think about more of it . . ."

"Captain!" the sentry at the barn door came over. "I think that prisoner is dead."

"Let's take a look," the captain answered.

They found Ed on his back and, though there was not a mark on him, there was no question about his being dead.

"Any suggestions, Lieutenant?" the captain asked, without special interest.

"A far-fetched one, sir," Rick said. "Is it possible for a man to die of fright?"

"Yes. It has been known to happen. Was this man such a physical coward?"

"He always was, sir."

"Well," the captain shrugged, "then the case is closed."

☆ 19 ☆

THE ARMY WAS ACCUSTOMED TO THE BELIEF THAT SHERI-
dan was indefatigable and indestructible. The men had seen
him at their evening fires, on the picket lines at midnight,
on the road before dawn and in the thickest of every fight.
Grant was active and fearless, but he was not omnipresent as
was Little Phil. Grant was given to long spells of brooding,
whereas his chief of cavalry did his thinking at top speed.
Now, when both leaders were straining every nerve to corner Lee's army, their characteristics were emphasized. Grant
was quiet as he chewed his cigar, Sheridan tore around on
Rienzi, shouting, waving his hat and urging everyone to go
faster.

Early in the morning, after the battle of Sailor's Creek,
he put his troops in motion toward Farmville, where Lee was
supposed to be. "Don't let them rest," he repeated over and
over as he rode among the columns. "Don't let them forage
or sleep or think what to do next. Keep after them!" He
spurred the big black horse on and on.

Sheridan was by no means the only one who was push-
ing the pursuit. Every Yankee in the ranks knew what was
at stake and was giving all he had to the effort. The cavalry
ranged far and wide toward the west, while the infantry

tore along both sides of the Appomattox River at a terrific pace. They had done some tall marching in their day, especially the Sixth Corps, but nothing to equal this. Some days they made better than forty miles with nothing to eat because the wagon trains were so far behind.

They were not supermen who went on uncomplainingly, they cursed and criticized and sometimes fistfights broke out when units tried to hog the road. But they kept going all day and all night, with only short periods of rest, and they grew so tired they slept on their feet, with no remembrance of the country they passed through. They fell out by thousands, but as soon as they could move again they picked up their muskets and went on. They knew it was their final test and that this road, cruel as it was, was the one they had hoped so long to see.

Lee's army was more heroic because it was suffering the same pace without hope. If it could reach the Danville Railroad it might struggle a little longer, but victory was out of the question. The splendid legions that had maneuvered so brilliantly in the past would never maneuver again. They were worn out. The marvelous thing about it was that those decimated regiments of starving men still kept to the road and struck back viciously when they were pressed too close. Grant wrote Lee urging an end to the sacrifice, but the old warrior would not bow his head. He led his men grimly toward the west, sharing their starvation rations and their despair, yet hoping in some vague way for a postponement of the end.

Early in the evening of April eighth Sheridan walked

over to a grove of oaks, where Ocean was feeding Rienzi his grain.

"What do you feed him, Pond?" he asked. "Grant has two horses, but they're not in as good condition as this one."

"This horse eats ground thunderbolts, General," Ocean answered. "It's the natural diet for Morgans."

"I almost believe you." Sheridan smiled. "Well, let him finish his supper, then saddle him up. Tie a couple of feeds to the saddle. He may have to eat on the run for a while."

"Yes, sir."

Sheridan stood looking at the sky. It was a beautiful twilight, warm and sweet with the scents of spring. It was so unusually quiet, despite the noises of camp, that frogs could be heard croaking beside the road.

"Tomorrow is Palm Sunday," the general said in a gentle voice. "Wouldn't it be wonderful, Pond, if the Saviour would ride into Virginia tomorrow as he once rode into Jerusalem!"

"Do you think it's that near the end, General?"

"It could be. Lee has given up trying to reach Danville and is heading for Lynchburg. If we can cut him off at Appomattox — Well, we shall see what we shall see. Where is O'Shay?" He was impatient again.

"He is asleep in his tent, sir."

"Tell him to report to me at once on a fresh horse."

"Yes, sir." Ocean went over and poked Rick with his foot.

"Go to blazes!" the boy mumbled.

"That's where you'll go, my boy, if you don't spring to. Phil Sheridan is waiting. I'll saddle for you."

Rick reeled to his feet. "No time to eat?"

"No. There's a big drive starting."

"How do you know so much?"

"Stop yapping, if you don't want to be blistered."

Rick was the only courier at headquarters. Sheridan had sent the others right and left to prod the weary infantry. Obviously this would be another night without rest.

"O'Shay," the general almost threw a sealed dispatch at him, "get this to Custer at the Appomattox crossing. Tell him I will follow soon."

"Yes, sir."

Rick leaped into the saddle as Ocean led his horse up. The road west was through heavy woods where darkness came early. It was rutted and littered with debris and clotted with traffic, but he galloped through, shouting, "Give way there, give way! A message from Sheridan! Give way!"

Sometimes in the past he had roared such orders just to show off his authority, but now he was in dead earnest. There was something tragic in the air, a sense of desperate urgency that must be obeyed. Custer was the one Sheridan sent in when he wanted a slapdash job done in a hurry. Rick found him by a campfire, leaning against a tree as though posing for a picture — wide-brimmed upturned hat, long golden curls, sweeping mustache, gold-braided jacket, yellow gauntlets, crimson sash, cavalier boots. A pistol butt showed in the top of the right boot, more pistols and a saber hung from his belt. Even when at rest the man could not help being spectacular.

Rick saluted and held out the message. "Compliments of General Sheridan, sir."

Custer read it, looked at his waiting officers and read it again.

"Yippeee!" he whooped and his handsome face lit up. "Boots and saddles, boys! Lee's supply trains are at Appomattox. We'll get them! We'll cork the bottle this time!"

Bugles sounded, coffeepots were kicked over, troopers ran for their horses, food and fatigue forgotten. This was the sort of thing they loved and they galloped away in the twilight after their show-off leader, who was superb at such a time. The Rebels were hit by surprise just as several railway trains started transferring precious food to a long string of waiting wagons. They were sitting ducks. The Yankees swarmed over them. After a brisk little fight they captured everything in sight: guards, trains, wagons, twenty-five field guns and all the supplies Lee had scraped together for his starving army.

Rick rode after Custer, yelling and shooting with the others. He knew there had been casualties but it didn't matter. This was a grand, smashing celebration and no one worried about getting shot. Some of the troopers were railroad men, and they took over the locomotives and went tooting and clanging and banging up and down the tracks until Custer stopped them. Fun was fun, but there was still a war going on. He ordered the trains run out a few miles and put under heavy guard so the enemy could not get at them, then, still thirsting for action, he started rounding up what fugitives he could find in the dark.

The road he followed led uphill through the woods, and at the top, in a clearing, he pulled up short. There was a barricade across the road and off in the distance were hundreds of campfires.

"There is Lee's army," he said in a strangely calm voice to those with him. "And we are west of it!"

The race was over. The tip of the Federal force had at last reached out between Lee and the western mountains where he had hoped to escape.

"Keep an eye on things here," Custer said to one of his officers. "I will find General Sheridan." He wheeled and galloped down the hill, unwilling to trust a courier with the news.

Meanwhile, Sheridan had collected most of the remaining cavalry and led it toward the railroad, where he hoped a crisis was shaping up. He and Custer met at Appomattox Station. They went up the hill for a look at the campfires. Yes, they agreed, it was all that was left of the Army of Northern Virginia. If during the night enough infantry could be brought up fast — fast — the business might be finished the next day.

Sheridan sent Rienzi flying down to the station and sent off the dispatch for which Grant, at nearby Farmville, was quietly waiting: Lee was in a desperate fix. Now was the time to strike! Without waiting for Grant's reply Sheridan rushed orders to every general in his command to march all night toward Appomattox Courthouse, the logical place to surround Lee. Hurry up-hurry up-hurry up!

When he had done this he calmly arranged his immediate needs. Half his men were thrown out facing the Confederate line and the rest camped along the railroad. They must get what sleep they could, though there would be no rest for him. The next few hours might see the end for which he had fought so long and so hard. His cavalry alone could not hold Lee when morning came. If Lee chose to fight, as he most certainly would, he might reach Lynchburg twenty miles west and the war might drag on through another summer. But if the Union infantry came up early in the day, even the genius of Marse Robert and the courage of his men would not be enough. Sheridan paced up and down during the night, waiting, waiting.

Before daylight he went down to his camp by the railroad and called his staff together. They had never seen him so tense, suggesting a spring tightly wound and waiting to be released. His voice was calm but so resonant it carried outside the tent, where Rick and the others were standing by for orders. With his usual clarity, he gave them the lay of the land as his scouts had described it. Two, disguised as refugees, had been over the terrain the day before. A mile north of camp was the Lynchburg road, the only highway by which Lee could escape. It wound in and out of woods along a rise of ground. After a couple of miles it slipped into a small valley and kept on through the village of Appomattox Courthouse. Around the village the Gray army was camped, partially protected by breastworks half a mile eastward.

There they were, said Sheridan, and beyond those hills, perhaps six miles away, the Second Corps and the Sixth Corps would be swinging along the Lynchburg road at this very minute. Ord's corps was already on the field behind the Blue cavalry and the Fifth Corps was close on the south. "So you see, gentlemen, we are on three sides of the enemy, infantry east and south of him, cavalry west. He cannot hope to escape north, so his only chance is to break the western line. The attack will come at any minute."

He broke off in the midst of a sentence and raised one hand. In the distance musket fire was crackling, then came the roar of artillery. The old battle light was in Sheridan's eyes. "Bring up your men, gentlemen, and bring them up fast!" He was out of the tent, leaping toward Rienzi, who was already saddled.

Once more the hungry troops picked up their muskets before the breakfast fires were kindled.

"Where's the grub you promised we'd get at the railroad?" one of Ord's men, who had marched all night, shouted to his captain.

"You'll get it later." The officer motioned him into line. "Breakfast can wait, but the war can't."

The infantry faced north toward the Lynchburg road, crowding along a little back road through woods so thick no one could see any distance ahead. The firing rose to meet them. They came out of the woods and surged across the main highway, swinging east to reinforce Sheridan's hard-pressed dismounted troopers.

"We'll get 'em!" an infantryman yelled to a wounded cavalryman who sat in a fence corner.

"Don't hurry," the trooper answered. "We've already done the fighting for you."

"We don't have to ride — we walk like men. We haven't eaten or slept for twenty-four hours, horse soldier."

"We haven't eaten or slept since the Battle of the Wilderness, straw foot."

They were so weary they were not quite sure what they were doing, but they marched on into the line of artillery fire. Sheridan was there, as they expected, smoke drifting around him and shells exploding over his head. The Rebels had scattered his outnumbered cavalry and, while it was trying to reform, the front was broken wide open. The Confederates went in with a yell, believing for a moment they were still able to do the impossible. Then the cheer and the hope died as they saw long lines of Blue infantry marching over the hill.

On the edge of the clearing, Rick saw the Federal lines spread out and out with more behind, moving inexorably to the last act. It was not that they were so numerous, but that the Confederates were so few. Of a sudden everyone who could see those Rebel regiments realized they were pitifully shrunken. The flags were there, as straight and proud as ever, but each seemed surrounded by little more than a color guard, the ranks were so reduced.

By common impulse the two armies stood looking at each other. The shooting nearly stopped, though no orders had been given. It was as though in this game each side was saying, the next move is yours. A great tableau was being imprinted on this page of history, yet few of the actors appreciated it. Both forces were too tired and hungry to have any highfalutin thoughts about the drama of the moment. The Yankees grumbled because they had been cheated out of their breakfast and the Rebels felt worse for not expecting any breakfast. They all wanted to quit and eat and sleep for a while, but they still feared each other. A Northern infantryman might have spoken for anyone on the field when he muttered, "Godfrey! I dread the moment when they open up on us again."

That moment seemed close at hand. Sheridan had not wasted a split second daydreaming, and now had his cavalry all mounted and in line toward the south, ready to hit the flank of the Rebels who had swung around to meet the force of Federals coming from the west. Grant was still on the road somewhere and Sheridan was in command on the field. Fate, or perhaps Grant, had chosen the ideal leader for the final blow.

The long blue lines of Ord and Griffin were moving again and the Confederate line was pulling back. Sheridan's troopers were poised, stiff in their saddles, the sunlight flashing on their drawn sabers. The tension could not endure.

It broke as a solitary rider galloped out from the Confederate ranks carrying a white flag.

Without waiting for orders, a majority of the Rebels began stacking their arms. They were through. The Yankees had dreamed for years how they would split the sky with cheers when it was ended, but now they sat down quietly. It was too much to handle all at once. Their first reaction was one of actual sadness as they looked across the open field at the men they had learned to respect. They were good men, Americans, who had been beaten in an honest fight. It had all been a mistake, that fight. There was nothing to cheer about. Let's all go home and get rested and start living again.

Phil Sheridan was not sentimental about it. When the Confederate officer announced that General Lee asked a suspension of hostilities pending negotiations, the little general answered stiffly that he would listen to no terms except surrender to General Grant as soon as that commander arrived. General Longstreet rode over from the Rebel lines with the assurance that Lee would surrender. With this Sheridan was satisfied, though he warned that none of the Southerners had better try getting away until things were settled.

Rick went about his duties in a half-daze, unable to realize the war was over. He had lived through the shooting and the sickness and would soon be free to — to what? It struck him suddenly that his future was blank paper on which he had no idea what to write. But that could wait.

Even Sheridan was waiting now. It was one o'clock before Grant rode into Appomattox Courthouse. He was covered

with dust, more stoop-shouldered than ever, with no suggestion of the conquering hero about him.

"How are you, Sheridan?" he asked in casual neighborly
fashion.

"First rate, General," Sheridan answered briskly. "The
Rebel army is over there in the valley. General Lee is waiting
to receive you in that little white house." He jerked a thumb
down the road.

"We will go over at once," Grant said. He looked down
at his dirty uniform and shrugged, then explained that his
dress uniform was packed away in a wagon somewhere.

Rick followed at a respectful distance. When he saw that
Sheridan, Ord and the others waited in the yard while Grant
went in to confer with Lee, he retired still farther and sat
alone by a fence. When the officers finally went inside, he
stayed where he was, thinking. Finally he saw Ocean in the
road and waved him over.

"How do you feel?" The older man pulled off a leaf and
chewed the stem.

"Numb. I doubt if I ever come to."

"In case you do, have you any plans?"

"Plans? No."

"What about keeping on in the cavalry? You like
horses."

"I like horses all right, but no more army for me."

"Do you mind if I talk to you?" Ocean spat out the
leaf.

"No." Rick looked at him curiously. "Fire away."

"You think I am a spy, don't you?"

"Well," the boy hesitated, "sometimes I have thought so."

"But you weren't quite sure."

"No. I was never quite sure what to think about you."

"Good!" Ocean smiled with one corner of his mouth. "That is just exactly what I wanted folks to think. The truth is, Rick, I'm sort of influential in the business world and I've been around and met quite a few people. But I'm not the society kind. I am a Vermont farm boy."

"Are we getting around to Justin Morgan again?" Rick laughed.

"We are." Ocean's blue eyes twinkled. "You see, Rick, when the war broke out they said I was too old to fight. Maybe so, but I knew I could make myself useful somewhere, if I could get away from the people who were fussing about my health. So — well — I closed out my business and disappeared."

"You ran away?" Rick asked incredulously.

"Sure, same as any boy. I went out West and joined the cavalry. I didn't go in for the real drill part, but I knew quite a lot about caring for horses — shoeing, doctoring and so on — so I fitted in. I enjoyed it, too. I have a passion for horses."

"But where do the Morgans come in?" Rick was still half-joking.

"Give me time. General Sheridan liked my work so, when he acquired Rienzi, he gave me the whole care of him. And he took me East when he joined Grant. I told him the whole story — you can do that with Sheridan — and made him promise never to promote me or mention me in any way. There are a lot of New Yorkers and Vermonters in the army and I didn't want to bump into them and have them try to have me discharged because I am overage. That gave me the reputation of being sort of mysterious."

"It certainly did," Rick agreed.

"When, just for the fun of it, I dressed up like a Confederate colonel and did a little spying for the general, some people got downright suspicious."

"And why not?" Rick felt his ears burning. "Can you blame me?"

"Not a mite."

"But I should have trusted you, after all you did for me. What can I do to make up?"

Ocean did not hesitate to answer that one. "Come to Vermont and help me. I am going to spend the rest of my days perpetuating the Morgan breed of horses. I have a dozen on my farm up there now. There is a future for Morgans and for those who love them. Will you come with me, Rick?"

"Will I!" Rick looked away, blinking fast. "Nothing could suit me better."

"Look!" Ocean whispered. "They are coming out."

General Grant and General Lee stood outside the front door of the little house and politely raised their hats to each other. Lee was resplendent in a braided uniform and shining sword. With the dignity and pathos of a fallen hero he mounted his horse and rode slowly down the road and out of the war.